Copyright ©2020 Tiffany & Sha

All rights reserved. This book or any portion thereof may not be used in any manner whatsoever without the express written permission of the publisher except for the use of brief quotations in a book review.

Tiffany Acknowledgments

Daddy Joseph Singleton-

You left me in this cruel world on 10/25/18. I love you with everything in my and I will forever miss you. Everything you taught me I will live by it. Everything I do I'm doing it for you and Terry. You're my angel now and I will always remember your last words to me and it will forever be engraved in my heart (I love you to baby.) When I feel like giving up I know I can always look in the sky and know you're watching over me. When I want to break down and cry I know you will forever comfort me even though you're not her physically. You have your wings now daddy. I miss you much, but I have to try to keep living, even though its hard I know you'll whoop my tail if I gave up. Rest peacefully daddy. -Your baby girl.

Goddaddy Terry Underwood-

May 24, 2009 you left me and I vowed to always make you proud. I know since then I have done nothing but make you smile in heaven. I know you and daddy living up. You have your best friend back with you now. Just know that I will always make you both proud. Rest peacefully goddaddy-

I would also like to give a special thanks to my cousin Tanya Boone. I love you big cousin, you're my angel now, watch over me.

. I would like to give a special thanks to my mother Ethel Burnett When others doubted me you to pushed me to be the best I could be, and I will forever be grateful for that. To my sisters Sha'Mara Scales and Callie Russell, thank you for being my role models and helping me set goals and achieving them all. A girl

. couldn't ask for a better support system.

-Tiffany Singleton

About Author Tiffany Singleton

Born and raised in Flint, I am the last child out of eight. Besides family, writing is the next important thing in my life. I started writing when I was just in the eighth grade around the same time my godfather died. Needing a way to express my emotions mostly anger and sadness I turned to writing poetry. Over the years I realized that I had a real talent when it came to writing and I started my first novel with was The Perfect sin, but the book that got noticed by Shameek Speight was Secrets From Within so that will always be a special book to me. Sadly, to say, last year October 25th I almost ended my writing career because I was going through so much. My dad died and he was one of my biggest supporters when it came to writing. He always told me "One day you gone write a million dollar book and you gone by me a new van". I would just laugh like I got you daddy and now I'm just stuck wishing I could have blessed him with that van before he passed away. Cancers a bitch. After listening to Jamie Fox song I wish you was here I realized I couldn't give up because I made it to fair and I still needed to get my name out here not only my name but the Singleton name. What Jamie fox say *"Everybody's calling my number everybody's calling my name but in the mist of it all I can still here you say son walk up right and straighten yo tie you don't want one of them good jobs to pass you by don't act no fool I'm watching you and now that you're gone , it still feels like you do."* This is the verse that made me continue writing. To my readers I love y'all and thank you for always keeping it real with me and supporting me even when I was ready to give up.

-Much Love Tiff,

Rest in love Daddy and Goddaddy

Acknowledgments

First and fourth most I would like to thank God for giving me the gift of life. I would love to thank my wonderful son Timothy Jr. You came into this world and showed me that I could be a better person. I would love to thank my two sisters, Tiffany Singleton and Callie Russell, my best friends. I don't know what I would be without you pushing me and giving the advice that I will always need. I would love to thank my mother. MY rock. This lady shows me every day the true definition of being a strong woman. She has given her all to me and my sisters and you are still putting us first. I would also love to give acknowledgement to my dad. My father always told me you are a very smart woman and you can do anything that you put your mind to. You told me that I didn't have common sense but book smarts, I was that girl. You left me the 25 of October 2018. I am still learning to live without, but you taught me the necessities I needed to survive and for that I will be forever grateful. I love you old man, rest easy and continue to watch over us

I dedicate this book to you. All of you. Words cannot explain the love and admiration that I have for each and everyone of you.

One Love

S. Burnett

About the author

Hello, my name is Sha'Mara Burnett. I am 31 years old and live in Flint, MI. I have my Bachelor's in Criminal Justice as well as my Master's in Public Administration. I love books. Reading is one of my favorite past times besides spending time with my family. My family is my motivation. My son is the highlight of my life. He makes me want to be a better person. My mom inspires me to be a great woman and always told me that I will succeed. My Father (god rest his soul) was my inspiration. He never let anything get in the way of living. He was always hurting but gave 110 percent on anything that he did. My sisters, I couldn't imagine life without them. Those are my best friends and they push me to succeed. I also love to write.

What started my love for writing was English class and having to write a poem that inspired us. I begin writing about school and the differences that occurs with the people. Pouring out my heart in a piece of paper made me want to continue. The love I have for writing is what keep me going besides my family. Writing takes me to another universe and for that it made me start putting my writings in to books. It made want to show my talent and give my readers a piece.

One Love

S. Burnett

Where we left off

Chapter 7 Quin

This Connecticut trip came sooner that it was supposed to. It took everything in me not to say fuck it because Trinity was not trying to let me go. She set in the bed and cried while I packed a couple of clothes for this three-day trip. After I drooped Trinity off, I hoped in the car with the boys and we headed to the airport.

"How you feel Sincere." I had to check on lil bro because I knew he was feeling some type of way about the shit that was going on. We were so worried about the girls that we honestly forgot that, that was his pops to.

"I'm good bro, I can't lie and act like I'm not pissed the fuck off though. I'm just so ready to get it over with so my sisters can get closure. Y'all worried about me, I should be worried about y'all. Y'all the ones about to kill y'all family for y'all women."

"To be honest, I kill anybody for my baby, Serenity my whole heart and anybody who fucking with her fucking with me and I hate being fucked with." Qua was serious as fuck when he said that and I felt everything that he was saying, because I'll lay anything walking for Trinity motherfuckin Black.

"I'll kill every muthafucka walking if that means Sophia, Quadir, Quincy, Serenity, Trinity, and Sincere is safe and I put that on my fucking life." Pops was a certified OG and people knew better than to fuck with him, Pops have killed people for less.

Jumping on that plane, I was hoping for a smooth ride. I hated planes but I couldn't drive and get there and back as quick as I would like. The plane ride was smooth, all of us lost in our thoughts. I couldn't wait for this shit to be over. Finally landing we headed to our hotel to check in. we were in the suit of the Madison Beach Hotel. This hotel was everything. We all had our own room and if I wasn't there to kill a motherfucka than I would definitely be coming back.

The information that was giving to us was a bank that Omar had frequented. Deciding to stake the bank out tomorrow we decided to chill and smoke a couple of blunts. Waking up the next morning. I ordered breakfast for everyone and woke them up. We had to be at the bank by 9 and it was almost 7:30. Looking at my phone I had a facetime from Trinity.

"Hey Baby, what you are doing up?"

"I couldn't sleep, I wish you was here with me." She pouted in the phone.

"Now you know, I had business to take care of lil ugly ass girl, just remember I'm doing this for you. How my baby doing."

"He is doing good. Moving around and shit. I couldn't sleep because he was just going everywhere. I believe he know you gone to."

"Put the phone by your belly… Hey lil man, daddy here. I can't wait to meet you. make sure you stay in there until I get back. Let mama get some rest." Trinity was smiling and holding her belly.

"He loves when you talk to him."

"I know baby, get some rest I have to get going, call me if you, sis, or ma need anything. No matter what. If y'all go somewhere make sure to take security."

"I know, now give me kiss." Puckering up my lips I kissed her through the phone and hung up.

"She got yo ass whipped bro. Bring yo lil sweet ass on, it's time to go." Qua walked out the room laughing. "Don't Worry about that one bro. I will suck toes and everything for her. She got a nigga out of his element and I can't even front.

Walking out the suite we jumped in our rental and headed to the bank. This was going to be a long day. Parking down the street we were able to see everybody coming and going. An hour later we were staked out in front of the bank passing blunts between the four of us.

"Pops, how did you and moms know the difference between me and Quin."

"Man, when you a parent you know. y'all lil bad asses was and still is my whole fucking world. But to answer yo question, Quin ass always wanted to be up under you Qua. You were like his fucking protector. I remember one-night Quin just wouldn't stop crying, we tried everything to get him to be quiet so he wouldn't wake you up. As soon as we put his spoiled ass in the crib next to you, he rolled over and fell right to sleep." Sincere was laughing and I just sat there and smirked because I knew my pops wasn't lying. My twin was my best friend and he acted like a second father to me even though his ass was only two minutes older than me.

"I knew this nigga loved me and shit. I hope my lil niggas close like me and bro." Qua turned around and gave me a dap. "Don't feel left out lil bro, you my lil bro to and I love yo ass to." He dapped Sincere up and turned back around. After being out there for hours we finally went back to the hotel and we were all pissed because we didn't find the nigga we were looking for. This nigga was hiding too good for me, but his bitch ass was bound to pop up sooner or later.

"Man Fuck this shit. I say we go home and just finish getting this baby shower stuff together. If we don't have this shit together, we going to have some mad ass women."

"I know, I just updated our tickets we can be out of here in a couple of hours. Grab everything and let's be out." Qua directed

After everybody grabbed their things they headed back to the airport. Deciding not to tell the girls. They wanted to sneak up on them and surprise them. The flight back home was easier than going. It was quicker and that's what I needed. Making it home at one in the morning. I took my shower and climbed in the bed with Trinity. We would go home tomorrow.

"Hey boo, what you are doing here." She rolled over and kissed me. That's how you know you love someone, kissing them with that stank ass morning breathe.

"We couldn't find him, but that don't mean we still not looking. Don't worry about its ma. The next week focus on you and Serenity.

Chapter 8: Serenity

"Daddy, your baby girl aint a baby anymore. I'm a grown a woman. Do you see my belly daddy, these boys are about to be the death of me. I can't wait to hold them and give them the same love you gave me. I promise you we're going to find the nigga that killed you, I won't have peace until I do. Daddy, your baby boy is so grown now, he looks just like you. Sincere Jr. I still can't believe that mom and Trinity parents did that to you. I hope you dancing in heaven daddy." Picking up my phone I started to play a song and sing to my daddy headstone. "Tell me what do it look like in heaven is it peaceful is it free like they say does the sun shine bright forever have your fears and your pain gone away cause here on earth it feels like everything good is missing since you left and here on earth everything different there's an emptiness ohhhhhhhhhhhhhhhh I hope you dancing in the sky I hope you singing in the angels choir and I hope the angels know what they have I bet it so nice up in heaven since you arrived." Kissing my finger, I placed my fingers on his headstone. "I would bend down and kiss you daddy, but I won't be able to get up. I love you and I miss you so much, continue watching over your baby girls and baby boy." Looking at the sky I smiled and when I looked back at his headstone there was a bird on it. "I knew you heard me daddy." Turning to walk away I hoped in the passenger seat and Qua leaned over and kissed me.

"Let's get you ready for your baby shower ma." Driving towards the house I seen all the decorations and it was set up so beautiful. Watching Trinity wobble to our front door had me smiling. My best friend was so freaking happy and if she was happy, I was ten times happier because seeing her happy made me happy.

"Y'all glam crew is already upstairs. Go get sexy." Quin kissed Trinity on the lips then kissed me on the cheeks.

"Why the hell y'all have them go upstairs, my fat ass not going up there these twins' boys aint gone let me make it up there."

"You always complaining, all them ladies up there set up and you want them to come down here." Quin ass always made something a joke, but I was dead ass serious, so I walked my big ass to the guest room and set down in the vanity. Not soon after our glam squad was coming downstairs and setting up.

When our hair and make-up was finally done, we were so freaking pretty, and it was hard for us to stop the tears from falling. I was beautiful but my best friend was so fucking beautiful.

"Trinity, now I see why Quin wife yo fine ass. Even with the big ass belly you still putting all these hoes to shame. I would hug you but my belly even bigger than yours and it won't work." Trinity laughed so hard when I said that. "I'm tired of all y'all laughing at me when I be dead ass serious. When I drop my babies imma start slapping y'all asses.

"Y'all are so beautiful." Sincere came in the room and hugged us both. "Pops would be so proud of y'all right now. I know baby showers are supposed to be for the babies, but I couldn't help but to buy y'all these." When he pulled out two necklaces with a small frame made with diamonds, I couldn't stop the tears from falling. Inside the frame was a picture of me, him, Serenity and our pops when we were younger.

"Damn, Sincere you made us mess up our makeup." Trinity was fanning herself to stop from smearing the make up even more.

"Y'all don't need that shit anyway." Walking up to both of us again he put the necklaces around our necks. "Everybody waiting on the entrance of the two Queens of the hours."

"Don't forget about the kings, a king aint shit without his queen. Y'all so fucking sexy man." Quin walked up and pulled Trinity towards him and Qua did the same to me.

"Damn, I can't believe you belong to me. I love everything about you. you're so damn beautiful ma."

"Well you better believe it daddy." Kissing him we made our way downstairs and into the back of the house. It was beautiful. The king crowns was placed all around the yard. The royal blue and gray were breathe taking. Taking my hand Qua led me to the chair as to where we would be sitting at. Since this was a co-ed baby shower the men had their friends there also.

Courtney walked to the front of the guest to start the games. "Okay ladies and gentlemen, we have a lot of prizes for these games. The first game will be for the women. We are going to see who can suck a baby bottle the fastest. The First one who finish the bottle will win a hundred dollars."

Grabbing the bottles, she started passing them out. "I'm playing to, Trinity you are playing." I asked while grabbing a bottle from Courtney.

"Now you know I am playing, even though we can't win." Trinity playfully rolled her eyes at Courtney.

"Bitch don't play, you just worry about sucking." Courtney yelled while walking fast away from her.

"I'm going to beat your ass."

"Everybody positions their selves. GO" Courtney started it off

"Damn bro these hoes not playing. Imagine what they could do to a dick. The way they are sucking these bottles." Quin tried to whisper to Qua, but I heard everything. He better shut up before Trinity kicks his ass. The baby showers were going off without a hitch. The food was amazing, so you know our big asses had 2 plates. We had greens, neckbones, BBQ, and we even had Mexican food because we couldn't choose.

Finishing up the food it was times for the gifts. Even though all three boys had something it was the thought that counted. Looking at the first gift it was addressed to all of us from Ma and pops. Opening the envelopes, it was 1000,000 dollars put in a trust fund for each of the boys. This money was going to be used for college. I understand that their fathers are dope boys but we trying to get them out the game so we know our children will have legit businesses also.

Trying to get up proved harder than it was. "Don't be trying to get up. We will come to y'all." Ma said when her and pops got up and came to where we were at. "Thank you so much." I had tears flowing down my face. I knew I was going to be crying by the end of the day. The boys received everything from money to shoes and clothes. Some of the clothes going to take them years to get into.

After the shower we made our way back in the house. Everybody was gone and now it was just me and Qua. After our shower we were lying in bed. "Thank you bay for everything. I can't wait to meet our boys." I kissed Qua and straddled him. It took a lil time, but I made it up on him. Feeling his dick hard underneath me, I knew what time it was. Thank goodness I wasn't wearing any panties. Lifting me up some I started rocking on his dick.

"oooohhhh baby you so big." Grinding on Qua I knew he was in his zone biting the beautiful lips made me twerk faster. "Ma you got that wet, wet." All of a sudden, I felt a burst of water.

"What the fuck bae, you just pissed on me." Qua looked at me like I was nasty. "Naw fool my water just broke."

"SHITTTTTTTT….IT…..HURTS." I was screaming as tears came from my eyes. Finally snapping out of it Qua helped me off him and both of us in the shower. Hurrying up we washed up and got dressed. It was time to meet of lil angels.

Quin

"Bae, get some clothes on Serenity water just broke." I rushed into the room to get Trinity because we had to get to the hospital ASAP.

"Okay here I come." Moving as fast as her belly let her move, she wobbled into our walk-in closet. "Oh, shit. Quinnnnnn."

"What's wrong baby."

"My water just broke."

"You got to be fucking kidding me. Let's get you in the shower." Grabbing her hands, I helped her in the shower and rinsed her off before she slipped some sweatpants and a big shirt on. After grabbing the baby bags, it took no time to get to the hospital and get her in the labor and delivery section.

After damn near begging and bribing the doctor, he finally agreed to let Serenity and Trinity have their babies in the same room. They were moved to a private room and the doctor called the best nurse from that floor to come and be their nurse.

"Ahhhhh, bae this shit hurt." Serenity had real tears falling down her face, from what the doctors said she was dilatated to five, so my nephews was almost ready to make their grand entrance.

"I know ma, it's almost over. Just think in a couple of more hours our baby boys will be here and you want have to walk around with that big ass belly." Qua laid his head on her belly and she rubbed his head before popping him in the head when she had another contraction.

"How you feel ma, you okay." Trinity was eating ice chips and she was okay because she was only dilated to two. My boy was stalling, I guess he didn't want to share a birthday with his cousins.

"I'm okay, I'm doing better than Serenity. Help me up so I can go and hold my best friend hand." After getting her up and on her feet, she went and set in the chair next to Serenity bed. "My nephews almost here sis, I can't wait to see them." Trinity kissed Serenity head and she bussed out crying.

"Trinity, it hurts so fucking bad. I'm never having another baby again. I'm done with this shit." After another hour it was time for Serenity to push.

"On the count of three Serenity, I want you to give me a big push. One, two, three." After pushing for damn near twenty minutes, my nephews Quadir Richardson Jr. and Nadir Richardson was finally born. Serenity was pissed at Qua because she blamed him for the pain that she was in.

"Congratulations bro." I hugged my brother because he had tears falling out of his eyes while he was looking down at his boys sleeping in the bassinet.

"Thanks bro you next."

"Whenever his ass stop being so damn stubborn. I think it's about to be soon because Trinity in a lot more pain now."

"Congratulations best friend, I can't believe, owwwwwwwww." I raced over to Trinity and held her hand while she was having a contraction.

I'm so fucking happy I'm not a fucking female man. I can't even imagine having to go through this type of fucking pain. "This shit hurt."

"I know ma, you see the pain yo best friend just went through." I kissed her head and walked over to pick my nephew up. They were the splitting images of me and Quadir, this shit was crazy.

"They look just like yaw. I hope they don't act like y'all." Serenity laughed but she was serious. Another Hour later me and Qua was sitting there holding the twins while Serenity slept. She deserved to sleep because my nephews were big as fucking and I know the ripped her the fuck open.

Next day.

"Pushhhhhhhh, ma." I was at the end of Trinity bed coaching her as I watched my junior come out.

"I hate you quin, why in the fuck did you do this to me." Trinity had sweat coming down her face.

"Oh my god, what the fuck. Yo pussy chocking the fuck out my son Trinity. I know yo ass betta fucking push." Quadir and Serenity was laughing but I couldn't stand looking at this shit.

"Qua, man how did you look at this shit twice. I'm bouta pass the fuck out." I started breathing hard, and almost started to cry with her when she pushed one more time and my junior made his way into the world.

Within twenty-four hours I became an uncle and a daddy and couldn't nothing in the world fuck up my mood. These boys could have been fucking triplets with the way that they looked. I knew we had trouble on our hands looking at the three of them sleeping in the bassinet. Yes, all three of them was in the same bassinet because they weren't about to have my son looking like a fucking loner.

"Get together so I can take some pictures of y'all. Grabbing the babies Qua laid his sons on Serenity chest and I laid my son on Trinity chest. Pops was just a taking pictures like he couldn't help himself.

Five hours later we started to accept visits from our family members. Everybody was cooing over our babies and it made a nigga feel proud.

"I heard y'all muthafuckas was looking for me." We looked up and met eyes with our fucking cousin Omar and he had two guns trained on us. Ain't this bout a bitch.

Pink Mimosa 3

Tiffany Singleton & S. Scales

Serenity

The day I had my babies really changed my life, four months later here I am standing at the graveyard looking at the gravestone of the man I loved the most. I can't believe he's not here to see the babies grow up. I know if he was here, I wouldn't be going through half of the stuff that I'm going through.

"I love you. I still can't believe you left me so early. I'd do anything to have you here with me again. Keep watching over me and the babies, everything that I'm doing is for you." Kissing my fingers, I placed it on the headstones and walked away." Getting in the passenger seat, I broke down and Trinity hugged me.

"It'll get better sister, I promise you it will." Before pulling off we made sure our babies were okay and headed towards my house. When we made it to the house Quin and Qua was seating on the balcony that was attached to his smoking room that was upstairs. I took a minute and just looked at my man, Qua knew he was a fine ass man.

"You good baby." Qua met me by the car to grab one of the twin's car seats.

"Yes, I'm okay, you know I always get emotional when I visit my dads' grave site." Kissing me on the lips I followed him into the house and got the babies out of their car seats.

"You ate today fat ass girl." Quin rubbed Trinity belly. Her ass found out she was four weeks pregnant at her six-week checkup.

"It's yo fault I'm pregnant. I can't believe I let yo ass talk me into fucking you when our baby was only two weeks old."

"It'll be okay, I want a big family anyway." Quin kissed Trinity again before he picked Quin Jr up. I swear our babies looked like triplets.

"Go put on y'all swimsuits and meet us outside." Quin and Quadir took the babies outside while we went to get dressed.

"Girl, the twins did yo body right. I can't believe yo ass got a flat ass stomach again. Not only that but look at this ass." Trinity popped me on the ass before running to the guestroom to get dressed. I put on my two-piece bikini Gucci swimsuit with my Gucci cover up and my Gucci slide. I laughed when Trinity ass came out with the same outfit just in Prada. Pulling out our phones we took a couple of pictures and I couldn't help but to rub her baby bump.

When we finally made it outside the men was in the pool with the babies and they were having the time of their life. I smiled looking at my Finance and my baby boys, before I joined them in the pool and started swimming with Trinity right behind me. After thirty minutes of swimming, I grabbed my babies while Quadir grabbed Quin Jr and watched as Trinity and Quin raced in the pool.

"Naw, yo ass cheated." Quin was pissed when Trin made it to the other side and back before him.

"Naw, baby I didn't cheat. I won fair and square baby. Just admit you lost to a pregnant woman." Trinity started twerking her big ass.

"Yeah, it's funny now wait until you drop our baby yo ass gone be pregnant again at yo six-week appointment and I'm going to be the one laughing." Trinity looked at Quin and bussed out crying, all of us just laughed at her ass because we were used to it. Her ass cried more than I cried when I was pregnant with the twins.

"Don't cry now baby girl." Quin kissed her. For the rest of the night we set around playing cards and swimming before Quadir jumped on the grill. We were trying to enjoy the nice weather before Fall came in a couple of months.

"Did you enjoy yoself today ma." Quadir came and set next to me and grabbed Nadir out my hands so I could breast feed Quadir Jr. This was our nightly routine, I fed the babies and he put them to sleep.

"Meet me in the shower when you get done putting them to sleep." I winked at him and walked away to our room. Starting the water, I made sure the water was the right temperature for both of us and stepped in.

"Siri play R Kelly Touchin."

"Playing R Kelly touching."

Baby, I wanna do something different tonight aight?

(Okay, what you wanna do?)

I want you to sing to me, while I sing to you, while we do this.

(Okay)

Touching you, touching me, sexual chemistry

Girl seems like your body's ready and I know you won't regret it

(Turn the lights down low ready to let my juices flow)

(Baby double lock the door, let's start right here on this floor)

Sounds like the perfect plan, we're seconds away from loveland

All you gotta do is take my hand, now tell me baby who's your man

(You babe)

Who

(You babe)

You

(I am your lady, our friends are gone perfect)

(Now come and take it baby)

  I felt a breeze, so I knew my man was getting in the shower. Turning around I looked at him and my mouth begun to water. Taking my index finger, I traced some of his tattoos before I threw my arms around him and kissed him deep.

  "Did you bring the baby monitor in here." I made sure before we got it popping in the tub.

  "Yeah, now what you gone do with that." He nodded down to his dick standing at attention. Without him even having to tell me, I backed him into the wall and dropped to my knees. Taking my right hand, I started to massage the base while teasing the head with my tongue. When I saw that he was relaxed I removed my hand and deep throated him, while looking him in his eyes.

  "Grrrr, ahhhhh fuck." Grabbing my head, he started to slowly fuck my face and I relaxed my throat and let my man take control. "Just like that ma." Taking control again I started going ape shit on his dick with my mouth. "Iight man, fuckk." Grabbing me, he picked me up and slammed me against the wall with my legs wrapped around his neck. I braced myself because I knew exactly what was about to happen. Grabbing his head, I closed my eyes as I felt his wet tongue massage my clit.

"Shittt, Right there Qua." Gripping my ass in his hands he started to massage it as his tongue went to work. He was licking me like he was trying to prove a point.

"Quaaaaa." I felt the familiar feeling in my stomach, so I started rotating myself on his face. Not long after, I started raining all over his face. "Fuckkk, okay, bae. Pleaseeee." He wasn't letting up as I felt myself cumming again. Not giving me time to recover he put me down, turned me around, and bent me over before slamming inside. Only thing I could do was moan because no words was coming out.

"Throw that ass back Ma. Don't give up on me now." Grabbing my hips he started fucking me like he was crazy. I knew my kitty was going to be sore in the morning, but it felt to good for me to tell him to stop. Slowing down his pace, he started to slow stroke me while pinching my nipples.

"Shitt, Qua. Ahhhhhhh." Tears started falling out of my eyes while and I started to cum all over him while he picked up his pace again.

"Grrrrrrrr." Slapping my ass, I felt him release inside of me, before grabbing me and sliding to the floor. I needed to get on birth control before I ended up like Trinity ass. After washing each other up we made it to our bedroom and got prepared to go to sleep.

"I'm about to go check on the babies than go on the balcony to smoke. You coming with me?" Nodding my head, I got out of bed and headed to the balcony with our pre rolled blunts.

Qua

Putting my baby to sleep, I couldn't help but to think about the day after my baby gave birth

"I heard y'all muthafuckas was looking for me." We looked up and met eyes with our fucking cousin Omar and he had two guns trained on us. Ain't this bout a bitch.

Taking my gun out the small of my back me and Quin both aimed at him.

"Nigga you knew we was looking but you picked the wrong day to show yo face."

"Naw bro it's the right day, his bitch ass is in the right place. He not going to make it to a room his ass going straight to the basement." Quin told his ass.

Looking at the girls they were scared as hell. I knew I had to diffuse the situation as best as I could. This was supposed to be a good day, but it ended like this. Sneaking and hitting the nurse button on the remote. The nurse came in.

"Don't worry bitch nigga we'll see you again." I told Omar as he walked away. "I need Serenity and Trinity discharge papers with no questions asked." The Nurse ran away to get what I asked for.

Hearing my babies crying on the monitor, I made my way to their room and took them out the crib and rocked them back to sleep. Making sure they were both back good I put them in the bed and went to lay down. Before I had a chance, I looked at my phone and it was a text from Quin.

Twin: Meet me at the warehouse tomorrow at noon. Drop Serenity and the boys off to ma.

Me: Bet

Waking up refreshed me and Serenity got the boys together and I dropped them off to my mother. She was doing better now that her cancer was in remission. Pulling up to the warehouse I seen other cars besides my brothers. So, I knew he sent a text to everyone. Walking in I seen King and Prince. I didn't even know they were back. dapping everybody up I made my way to the head of the table where Quin was at.

"So, what's so important I had to get out bed and meet y'all ugly ass niggas." They all laughed. We had a good relationship with each of our workers.

"Bro, we got wind of Omar being around town. He was last seen on the northside with this woman. I got the address and everything. We riding out later so the girls and the kids going to have to spend a night over there. We gotta be focused on killing this nigga once and for all."

"That's cool. It's going to be some bitching and nagging but it's for their protection." Looking at King and Prince, "So how shit going up there?"

"We went in there and took over. We have some men that's working with us. Money is good and there's no beef as of right now." King said

"Yea we doing good, but we heard about everything that happened when y'all kids was born, by the way congrats. When we heard that shit it was no questions asked, we made our way back down for the night. We leaving again soon." Prince said

Seeing that it was still early enough we asked all our lieutenants was everything good on the work front. We had to make sure they had the product and wasn't nothing or nobody giving them problems. Seeing that everything was good we decided to meet back here at nine before we rode out.

Going back to the house was easier said than done. Ma, Serenity, and Trinity all got in our shit. We had to promise we was making preparations to get out the game soon. It was not just me and twin no more we both had families and needed to be here for them. Since everyone was chilling, we decided to grill some lobster tails and some shrimp with a seafood salad.

Making sure that my babies and Serenity was good me and Quin left out the house to finish this business. Once we made it to the warehouse everybody was there and dressed in all black. "Alright niggas let's go put in this work." Jumping back in the car we made our way to the north side where Omar was staying. All the lights was off, so we had two men stay at the front just in case he tried to make a run for it. going to the back we twisted the knob and was open. What kind of shit was that? People was dumb as shit. Walking in the house we heard soft music playing and sounds of a bed knocking. This house was filthy. "Man, what kind of shit is that the roaches trying to get away." Quin said making everyone laugh. Walking further in the house down the hall we came to the door that we heard the music playing.

Busting the door open we came face to face with a fucked-up surprise. "Man, I know yo ass not in here getting yo booty tickled?" I just had to ask. This nigga acted hard core but he ass was sweet as pie.

Seeing him getting up we all trained our guns on him. "You thought we was going to let that disrespect happen?"

"Naw, I knew it was only a matter of time."

"Good." Quin said while letting a bullet go straight through his forehead and one to the heart.

"Damn nigga I had some questions to ask him." I told Quin before giving his partners two to the head.

"I couldn't take it bro, how the hell am I going to un-see that shit. MY EYES."

"Nigga shut yo dramatic ass up."

Easing out the house as quick as we came, we dapped up our people and told them we will give them something for they time later in the week. After showering and burning our clothes we made our way back to our parent's house. It wasn't no sense and waking them up.

Getting in bed with Serenity, "Is it handled baby?" Putting my arms around her she rested against my chest and got comfortable.

"Yes, you don't have nothing to worry about."

"Thank you, baby." She kissed me and went back to sleep.

Trinity

"Ayeeeee fuck it up bitch." I was standing in Serenity dressing room getting dressed while she was bouncing her big ol ass to Megan thee stallion and moneybag Yo new hottest joint *All That."* Best friend *WHAT YOU DOING WITH ALL THAT."*

"Ouuuuu nothin." She stopped dancing for a minute and came over to help me put my necklace on. "You're so fucking beautiful best friend."

"What y'all gay asses in her doing." Quin walked over to me and leaned his tall ass over me and kissed me on the lips.

"You know, I'm just watching my best friend bounce her big ol ass. I see why yo twin can't get enough of her. Look at their asses." We both turned to see Qua was basically drooling over Serenity. I loved they relationship man. "We wanna be like y'all when we grow up." Me and Quin laughed when they finally came up for air.

"Bro you getting soft on me. you almost took lil sis lips off her fucking body. You not hitting the blunt lil ugly ass boy." Quin was always cracking jokes and that's what I loved the most about him.

"Boy shut up, yo ass almost sucked the air out my lungs through my pussy and you want to talk to him about kissing his woman." I put my man on blast while Qua and Serenity doubled over in laughter.

"Keep that blunt bro, Imma go get my own. I don't want to taste my best friend juices and shit." Serenity took off running with Quin chasing her. I swear they was literally like sister and brother.

"Qua what the fuck we gone do with them." I shook my head laughing.

"I don't know lil sis. That's yo man and yo best friend."

"You right but you got it worse, that's yo woman and yo twin." Laughing I stuck my tongue out at him and we walked out the room to go find these childish ass partners of ours.

Walking in the kitchen they both were sitting at the bar throwing back shots.

"Trinity you want one girl." She through another shot back and bused out laughing.

"Keep playing with my girl ima have my twin bro to shoot the club up. I think you can go for a baby gi--. You know what never mind I can't even deal with yo ass we don't need a baby Serenity." Quin started shaking his head with his sexy ass face frowned up.

"Boy fuck you. Trinity why you keep looking in the mirror, girl you fine. If I was gay, I would definitely fuck." I spit the water out that I was drinking cause this girl was really fucking crazy.

"I really think y'all used to fuck before y'all found us." Qua walked up to Serenity and took the shot out her hand. "You getting carried away ma you still gotta breast feed my sons.

"We did you wanna see us kiss? Bae, I pumped enough for tonight to have a lil fun." She took the shot back out Qua hand, but he knocked it down breaking the glass.

"You had enough." He kissed her than slapped her on the ass. "Bro lets head out. Y'all good right." Nodding our head, the men walked out leaving us alone.

Serenity

Walking into Pink Mimosa, I was in my element. I remember shaking my ass on that stage making hella money, if it wasn't for Qua hating ass, I would still be doing it. It is not like I didn't have the money, but it was something about having motherfuckers drooling about what they couldn't have.

"What up boss?" My security asked. Giving him a head nod, I made my way back to the dressing room and looked at my strippers. I wasn't gay by a long shot; I loved some big black angus beef, but my ladies had that type of body that put buffy the body to shame.

"Hey girls" I waved at them to let them know I was in attendance tonight. Sometimes you had to sneak in to make sure the work was still getting done. Trinity and I was meeting here to go over our paperwork for the month. We had to make sure they strippers was tapping out and that the bar balanced with as much liquor as we ordered.

"Hey Bitch," I looked at Trinity as she waddled her ass in the office. It would be my best friend that found out she was pregnant when she went to her six-week checkup. Damn bitch didn't even get a chance to snap back. She was now four months pregnant and we were hoping for a little girl. It was enough men around we needed our princess.

"Bitch I'm tired Quin didn't want to let me leave the house." She sat down beside me and pulled out her apple laptop. Pulling up our files we engulfed in friendly conversation while we entered the information. Making sure we had everything we needed, we cut the checks for the bottle girls, bar tenders, cooks and security. Hearing a knock on the door Trinity yelled for who it was to come in.

Looking at the familiar face. "What's good boo?" I asked Sapphire giving her the opportunity to sit down.

"Well I wanted to tell you before the nosey ass bitches come to y'all. I'm a little over three months pregnant. I want to take leave until I have my baby." She looked at us and I could see her look Serenity in her eyes. We had a policy of making sure the strippers were able to come to us and discuss any problems they all had our work email, and they could contact us.

"That will be acceptable I understand the need to have a complete life outside of making money." You can return after the birth of your child. You will still be compensated 500 a month until you have your bundle. We know that's not enough, but it will help you some." I explained to her. Thanking us she got up and headed out the office.

"Bitch, Pregnant? I didn't even know she had a man." Trinity looked at me and laughed.

"Girl, I know. Let's get out of here and get dinner." Walking out to the club we decided to go to Red Lobster because Trinity pregnant ass wanted some of their biscuits. After spending some much-needed time with my sis I went home to cuddle with my man.

"Hey love, where you be?" I walked in the house kicking off my spiked black red bottoms.

"I be in the den." Qua sexy ass walked out the den with nothing on but those grey sweatpants. I immediately noticed that dick print. My mouth started salivating anticipating making it hit the back of my throat. He walked up and grabbed my head sticking his tongue so far in my mouth we became one. That was my man and couldn't nobody tell me different. Breaking the kiss, I asked where the twins was at. After he told me they were already put to bed I dropped down to my knees and pulled those sweats right along with me. Grabbing hold to his thick meaty dick I licked to tip and made it jump. Taking the whole thing in my mouth I made sure to make sure my mouth was super wet. Grabbing on his balls I started rotating them between my hands. Grabbing my head, he started to fuck my face and I relaxed my throat letting him go at it. Hearing his toes popping I knew he was coming and like the good fiancé I was I opened up wide and caught all them kids and swallowed them.

"Damn bae you must want something."

"Naw boo, I'm good I just wanted to satisfy you." Making my way upstairs to our bedroom I started to strip. Getting my water ready, making it hot as I can stand it, I got in the shower. Not even five minutes later I felt a gust of cold air and I knew my baby was about to rock my world. Going at it for about an hour we finally washed up and made our way to the bedroom. Laying on his chest I knew I found heaven.

Qua

My baby was the truth, you can't tell me nothing when it comes to Serenity. I didn't know how I was going to tell to tell her that me and Quin had to go to Flint for about three days. She was going to get pissed. She knows I have business there, but she wanted me to be fully legit. What she doesn't know is I plan to pass these streets on to King and Prince, but I need to make sure they ready.

Hearing her snore, I reached over and text Quin letting him know to meet us at our favorite breakfast spot to tell the girls about our upcoming plans. Pulling Serenity close to me I wrapped my arms around her and went to sleep.

The sun woke me out my sleep and Serenity were not in the bed with me. Looking at the clock I realized that it was ten in the morning. Hopefully she had the twins dressed we only had one hour before having to meet with them. Getting up to handle my hygiene I texted Serenity to make sure she had the kids ready she said she did and they she was in the twin's room. I know I could have just gone to find her, but I was being lazy.

Finishing up my shower I decided on my true religion black pants, with the shirt to match and my all black Jordan's. Wanting to be comfortable.

"Aye bae, I'm ready." She walked out the room with the twins. I guess great minds think alike she had the boys dressed in the same thing I had on and she was rocking the same but more feminine. Kissing her I took one of the boys and we made it downstairs to her black on black Jeep. Strapping the kids in we were on our way.

"Where we going babe?" Serenity asked while she was scrolling on her phone. I looked over at her and licked my lips. My woman was so fucking sexy, she had me wanting to pull this fucking Jeep over and fuck her on the side of the road.

"We going to meet Trin and Quin at breakfast we have some things that need to be discussed." Putting her phone down she looked at me. I knew her ass was about to cuss me out and she don't know nothing about what I am going to say.

"Why you couldn't you just tell me at home. It must be something that is going on because you usually would have told me by now. It's cool though, it bet not be nothing stupid or I'm going to shoot your dumb ass. Now play with me if you want to."

I had to do a double take, she never went off on me like that. I couldn't even say shit. I was just quiet the rest of the ride. Making it to our destination we got out the car and they was already waiting on us. Walking in the restaurant the hostess leads us to our table and we got all the babies highchairs.

After taking the orders, the waitress walked off, I guess Serenity couldn't hold it no more.

"Now what y'all fuck niggas got to tell us?" She looked back and forth between us with a scowl on her face.

"Now alright sis. Now you now we love you but ain't shit fuck nigga about us. You didn't know real until we came through."

"What the fuck ever, now Qua don't make me ask again?" She looked at me and I guess I couldn't stall no more.

"Quin and I have to go to Michigan for about a week."

"WHAT THE FUCK YOU MEAN YOU HAVE TO GO TO MICHIGAN FOR A WEEK. I'M PREGNANT WITH YO FUCKING CHILD AND I HAVE A FUCKING CHILD TO TAKE CARE OF BUT YO ASS WANT TO LEAVE. I SWEAR YOU GOT ME SO FUCKED UP QUIN." Trinity went in on my bro while me and Serenity set there watching the scene unfold. Serenity wasn't even mad because I guess she thought Trinity went off enough for the both of them.

"Trinity, I know yo ass betta take all the fucking bass out yo fucking voice. I told yo ass I had moves to make for me to get out the fucking game. NOW TELL ME WHAT THE FUCK YOU WANT TRIN. YOU WANT ME TO HANDLE MY SHIT OR STAY HERE WITH YOU."

Silence

"ANSWER MY FUCKING QUESTION." Quin was going off and Trinity took off running out the building as fast as she could.

"You fucked up muthafucka. I love you like a fucking brother but when it comes to Trinity, I'll fuck yo black ass up. Bae, get yo fucking bro in check." Serenity snapped on Quin than walked out the building after Trin.

"What the fuck just happened?" I looked across the table at Quin.

"I don't know but I think this crazy ass fucking girl left me."

"I guess yo stupid ass gotta ride with us cause Trin pulled the fuck off. I'm ready to fucking go. Bring y'all dumb asses on." Serenity slapped a hundred on the table and was about to walk out until I grabbed her by her arm.

"I don't know who the fuck you thought I was but you betta lose yo attitude right fucking now. You aint Trinity and I damn sho aint Quin. Watch yo fucking mouth ma." I was so close to her ear that only she could hear me, but I know she heard me loud and clear. She snatched away from me and walked out the door.

"Nigga if you got me in the dog house before I leave my woman for a week I'm fucking you up myself." Quin brushed me off and followed me out the door after we grabbed the kids.

"You betta call Trinity back cause it aint enough room for you in my Jeep." I gave Serenity a look and she shut the fuck up, while Quin jumped in the back seat holding his son.

"I'm taking you home bro." Quin nodded and leaned his head back against the seat.

Pulling up to Quin and Trin house, Quin Black Charger was in the driveway, so we knew Trinity was already home. After dapping my brother up, I made sure he got in the house before I pulled off.

"Why are you going to Michigan?" That's why I loved my woman because she waited until it was just us before she started to go in on me.

"On our thirtieth birthdays we giving the game up. The niggas who we giving the streets to live in Flint. We have to go scope the scene out to make sure this what we really want to do. I'm doing this for you and them two little boys in the back seat."

"Just come back home to me in one piece. You got one week to be in Flint before I come up there bussing my fucking guns."

"Alright then mama." Leaning over she kissed me on the cheek. "I love you ma."

"You can show me how much you love me when we get home. You gone let me water yo beard."

"You got it mama." I put the peddle to the metal trying to get home so my girl could give me some of my favorite juice.

Quin

When I walked into the house it was a little too quiet for me. I found Trin the in room laying across the bed holding her stomach.

"Did you really fucking leave me and our child at the fucking restaurant? What the fuck is wrong with yo ass." The way she looked at me would have had me scared if I was some bitch ass nigga. "TRINITY, I ASKED YOU A FUCKING QUESTION."

"Yo brother was there he wasn't going to leave you, so I left. Did that answer yo fucking question." Walking up to her I snatched her off the bed and shoved her against the wall.

"What the fuck is yo problem."

"My problem is, I'm pregnant and yo ass taking off to a whole different fucking state and I also have a fucking son to take care of. I wish I was a fucking daddy and could take off whenever the fuck I wanted to." Looking at her I took a step back and just stared at her.

"What the fuck are you saying. Are you saying that I'm not a good father. I take care of you and I take care of my fucking son. How the fuck you gone come at me like I'm a fucking dead beat." I couldn't even front like I wasn't hurt. "I'm a good ass nigga Trin, I don't know if its yo hormones or what but fuck you ma." Walking out the room I went to kiss my son and walked the fuck out the house. I had to get away from Trin before I snapped her fucking neck.

Jumping in my car I headed for a hotel because I didn't even want to be around nobody right now. All I wanted was to be inside my girl all night but here we are fucking arguing over some stupid shit.

"Welcome to the Hilton, do you have a reservation with us today." This little bitch was flirting with me and I wasn't in the mood.

"Ma, my eyes are up here, stop looking at the fucking print in between my legs." Her light skin ass turned red. "I need your best room for the night."

"Yes sir, how will you be paying today." Now she wasn't even looking me in the eyes.

"Card." Taking my card and License out I slid it across the desk so she could get me took care of.

"Enjoy your night. Let me know if you need anything." I shot her a smirk and went to the elevator. If Trin didn't have my fucking son I would have cut my fucking phone off but sense my son came first I left it on.

Walking into the penthouse I stripped down and made my way to the shower. Adjusting the water to my liking I step in and let the water run down my head. I felt like a lil bitch when the tears started streaming down my face. Now I know I'm not a bitch but what Trinity said to me hurt. After washing my ass with this lil ass soap that was given to you by the hotel, I stepped out the shower and turned the TV to ESPN catching the highlights until sleep found me.

Waking up I was delirious to where I was until I remembered what Trin ass said. Her ass didn't even call to see if I was ok last night. Grabbing my phone and seeing I was only at 10% I texted Qua and told him I would be there by one so we can get on the road. Grabbing my clothes I put them on and made my way to the house. Trinity was gone so I stepped in and took another shower before packing my duffle and getting dressed to make my way to get Qua.

Making it to Qua house I blew the horn and waited till he came out. Popping the trunk, he put his bag in and made his way to the driver side. My twin knew I couldn't stand driving that far plus I needed to roll up.

"Why you look so stressed bro and what the hell happened when you went home yesterday." He adjusted his seat and backed out while I rolled two blunts. We usually share blunt but I needed my own so I rolled him his own to. When he seen that I was rolling two blunts he shook his head. "Start talking bro."

"Do you think I'm a good dad and a good nigga to Trinity? This bitch had the nerves to basically call me a deadbeat, talking bout some fucking "*I wish I was a fucking daddy and could take off whenever the fuck I wanted to*" Bro you know it take a fucking lot for me to cry and this bitch had me in the shower crying like a fucking bitch. I hated that shit man, I couldn't even stay home last night because I was liable to take her fucking head off." My eyes were watering again and I was pissed at myself for letting her have me this fucking upset.

"First thing first fix yo fucking face. Never let a bitch make you feel less than what you really are. You a good ass nigga bro. You take care of yo woman and you take care of yo seed. Trinity ass was mad yesterday and she took it out on you but she know what she said was some bullshit. I need you to focus on the task at hand bro we almost out the fucking game. That should be enough for you to be happy as fuck right now." Lighting his blunt I handed it to him than did the same to mines as we hopped on the highway headed towards flint.

"You right Qua, you right. I hope Trinity think about what the fuck she said while I'm gone because if not, I'm going across her fucking head."

Qua laughed because he knew I was serious as fuck. Our mom taught us to never hit a woman, but we can knock a bitch out.

"Most fucking definitely bro, I need you to get yo mind right." The rest of the way to Flint was silent besides the music that was playing. We were both in our own thoughts, I'm pretty sure his thoughts was on giving up all he knew and my thoughts was on me possibly coming home to no woman. But fuck that if me and Trinity don't work, my black ass not getting out the fucking game.

"And I know what ass over there thinking, if something happened to you and Trinity, yo ass still getting out the fucking game nigga." Looking over at Qua I just laughed at his goofy ass, this twin shit was irritating because we really knew what one another was thinking,

"Fuck you nigga." Laughing he pulled up to this nice ass house on the outskirts of Flint in a city name Grand Blanc. "This shit nice as fuck." Qua nodded his head in agreement.

Reaching over he pressed the intercom and the big ass gates opened up so we could drive in. When we made it to the front of the house our niggas King and Prince was standing on the porch looking like some real hood ass niggas. Stepping out the car we both stretched and went to dap our niggas up.

"My niggas Qua and Quin what's up with it." Before we could answer a big ass black panther walked onto the porch and me and Qua jumped back fast as fuck while them niggas stood there laughing. "Princess down girl, they cool people. Go give them a kiss." I'd be damned if this big bitch didn't come and lick me and my fucking brother.

"Yo Quin, book some fucking rooms at a hotel cause I'll be damned if I stay in this damn house with a fucking panther."

King

"Whats good my niggas, how was that drive." I dapped them up while they ass was almost running from princess. Qua seemed to be cool but that nigga Quin was liable to kill my baby.

"Come on now niggas we will put her up." Prince told them so that they can bring they ass in the crib. Turning around we made our way back in. While prince put princess up, we went to the man cave. Grabbing two waters I gave it to them. "So y'all staying here or what, my ole lady cooking us a meal fit for a king. We have the room if you want to."

"Yea we will stay here, just keep that mean bitch away from me." Quin said while looking around.

O Shit let me introduce myself. I'm King, Last name don't matter right now just know ever since Qua and Quin told me and lil bro Prince to come here we had the streets on lock. We stepped on some toes to get where we at but we some thorough niggas. I am 25 years old and I'm what niggas would consider a motherfucking OG now. I have a beautiful wife name Kenzie. We been together for three years and married for two. We are having a beautiful baby girl name Karisma. My wife is seven months pregnant. These two ladies have my heart that's why when I moved here, I knew I had to have them in a secure place. Hence why we have princess.

Now me I am a what bitches would call a chocolate god with a big anaconda that knows how to work that motherfucker. I would have bitches walking with a limp once I'm done but luckily for my lady she the only one that gets blessed with it. I have dreads that I wear pulled back in a pony tail or have them twisted to the back. I'm tall about 6'6 with a solid 250 muscle body. Just know I'm that nigga.

"Hey baby Dinner is ready." She said on the intercom and had me snap out of my thoughts. Getting up I motioned for the fellas to follow me. Making it to the kitchen my baby had the spread already on the table. Sitting down we all was ready to start grabbing until we heard her mouth.

"Now I know three grown ass man did not just come to my table without washing their hands and wasn't going to pray. I know y'all better get up and handle y'all business. The food won't run away.

Getting up we all went to handle our business and we came back to the table and bowed our heads while Kenzie prayed over the food. She had lobster tails, shrimp, shrimp alfredo and crab legs. She also had steak. My baby threw down in the kitchen.

Having general conversation because we never talked about business in front of her. We finished eating and Kenzie got up and went upstairs while us fellas cleaned up and made sure everything was put away.

"Alright niggas we will get up with y'all later. Any room on the upper floor you can get. We riding out in the morning at ten so we can show the work we been putting in." Dapping everyone up I made it to my master suite. This was my piece. Even though this was our room she let me have the decorating part. It was fit for a King and Queen and I made sure that we had nothing but the best.

Kenzie was walking out the bathroom and I couldn't do nothing but stare. She didn't have no towel or anything on claiming she likes to air dry. "Hey boo, you can stop drooling now." She said to me. I couldn't help but stare. My wife was beautiful. Standing at 5 foot 5. She was slim thick, and the baby didn't do nothing but give her more ass, hips and breast.

"You just wait a minute let me take this shower so that I can make that kitty purrrr." Going in the bathroom I stripped fast as I could. Couldn't let her wait to long she will fall asleep in a drop of a dime. Hurrying up I washed and scrubbed my body with that Doves men and got out. Walking out the room she was laying on her back lightly snoring. Pushing her legs apart I licked up and down my heaven on earth. Taking her clit in my mouth lightly sucking made her squirm a little. By now she was dripping wet. Attacking her pussy with my mouth made her wake up and put push my head in deeper. I knew she was on the brinks of coming. Seeing her legs shake I didn't give her a chance to catch her breath before I pulled her to the end of the bed and pushed deep into her. Hearing her gasp. I knew I had her where I wanted her. Pulling those long deep strokes taking her breath away.

"ooooooo , Baby you feel so good." She told me. Turning her around I made sure she had the perfect arch well as good as that belly would let her. "Throw that ass back baby." Slapping her ass making it jiggle. She was throwing it back on my dick and I had to hold on for dear life. Who ever said that pregnant pussy is the best I need to give they ass a mill cause they never lied. Feeling her cum again I knew I could finally let loose. Filling her with my seeds, I had to make sure I didn't put my weight on her. Getting off the bed I went to wet a towel and cleaned her up then took care of myself. By the time I made it back to the room she was back sleep. Snuggling up next to my lady I pulled her close and rubbed her belly until sleep took over me.

"Nigga what kind of fucking mattress you got on the fucking beds I need to text Serenity right now and tell her to order that bitch." I couldn't even answer him cause when Quin came out in something that was identical to what Qua had on I laughed hard as fuck.

"Let me find out y'all two grown asses still dress alike. I can't believe this shit." Me and prince was literally doubled over laughing.

"Quin what the fuck man." Qua couldn't help but to laugh with us. "Y'all think I'm playing but when I tell y'all this shit comes natural it do. Being an identical twin something serious."

"Nigga I promise I didn't even know you had this same shirt in black." Quin through his arms around his brother shoulders and Prince did the same to me." Pushing his hand off me I walked off with Qua following me.

"Nigga little brothers irritating as fuck." Qua was only a couple minutes older than Quin so he considered his self the big brother.

"Black ass boy you only a couple minutes older than me shut the fuck up." Quin walked past me and Qua and jumped in the passenger seat of his car.

"Nigga what the fuck, we not driving a long distance get yo ass in the drivers seat."

Jumping in the car with niggas was going to be an enjoyable day. These niggas just woke up and had a nigga bout to die from laughing. Seeing that Qua got in the back seat I jumped in the front so I could show Quin where to go. Pulling out the gates we headed to dirty ass Flint. Where niggas get stabbed and shot for looking at you wrong. These niggas here wasn't on no playing.

"Damn niggas. We didn't say the hood hood. You could have least posted up in the semi-hood." Qua said as we pulled up to our trap on Ruth Ave. Parking behind this big blue house. We got out and made our way to the back door. Unlocking the door, we went inside and went to the basement. We had bitches down there bagging up our shit. Naked as the day they were born. We didn't trust a soul and bitches would hide that shit and sell for their selves.

"A niggas these the niggas right here you should be thanking for eating. Without them you would still be sitting in yo mama basement dreaming of that green shit." Prince told all the niggas we had in the basement.

Taking Qua and Quin upstairs after introducing them to everyone. We made our way to the main room where you had to have special security sequence to even get in. Doing our codes and putting our eyes to the display the steal door popped open. In this room was where we had more kilos at and where we stashed some of the money. This was just a lil place other than our warehouse. Since this was our main trap and we did more business than Walmart on black Friday in one day. After showing them the books and the money, we made we was on our way. Stepping to the front in the living room was where the fiends got served without opening the door. We had a slot where we can see them, but they couldn't see us. You could never be too careful.

In this short amount of time we had some officers on our payroll but, a nigga needed more government officials. I was making my way to that area soon. Going outside we walked to the front of the house coming down the street was this nigga Ace. He was known in these parts. He was on this side before bro and I took over. This nigga been butt hurt ever since. He started slowing down the car and I instantly pulled my hammer out causing these other three crazy niggas to do the same. Speeding up he got the hell off my street.

"Now who the fuck was that?" Quin asked while tucking his gun back in. Being street niggas, we kept a couple guns on us.

"This nigga who we took these streets from." Prince said. "But fuck him we going to Club Ocean tonight."

"What the fuck is a club Ocean" Quin asked

"That's where the bitches be twerking, with nothing on but pasties and always wet."

"Yea shit we there."

After making the rest of the rounds and showing them the warehouse, we went back home to get ready for the night. My wife trusted me, so I knew she didn't care that I went to see strippers.

Prince

Getting out our car and walking up to the door we were already hood celebrities. Dressed in nothing but the finest you know we all had on black and we stayed strapped.

"Now I know why they call this bitch Club Ocean, its not cause they wet these bitches smell a little fishy." Qua said while fanning his nose and walking to our section. We couldn't take his ass nowhere. This nigga always had some fucked up shit to say.

Making it to the section we had the bottle girl to bring our signature drink of Black Hennessey. These bitches were not that cute but they bodies was sick. Having a couple of them come up to our section. Ass was going everywhere, and these bitches was loving it. Dropping money on them we were in a zone.

"Now coming to the stage, Ms. Pretty Kitty cause when a nigga see it she make 'em purr." The DJ announced the next girl." This bitch came out dressed in all black with purple pasties on her tits dropping down to the floor she crawled to the edge of the stage, turned around and bounced her fat ass. Just looking at her you can tell she had an invisible waist. I was wondering how her waist was holding up her ass. Turning into a split I seen her ass had a mind of its own. She was bouncing them cheeks making this nigga Quin salivate.

"Damn nigga stop drooling." I looked toward Quin and he couldn't take his eyes off her.

"Nigga, I'm never pressed but when she gets off that stage, she has to come see me. I need to see that ass personally."

This nigga was going to get in trouble. I could see the light in his eyes. Trinity going to whip his ass. That girl is real life crazy. Not paying his ass no more attention I turned to my bros and them niggas was just sitting there. These married ass fools.

"Aye bro, we out. I had Kenzie come get us. This not our seen no more." King told me.

"Man, y'all old grandpa ass niggas."

"Whatever lil nigga just get home safe."

Making sure they got out the club safe me ad Quin finished with these bitches in here. "Aye lil mama." I seen this fine ass dark chocolate bitch. "You really taste like what you look like. "

"Why don't you take me home and find out. I will be worth your while."

"Alright go do what you have to do and meet me at the back door and bring Ms. Kitty with you."

She walked off putting a little extra switch and her hips. That ass was just moving like crazy.

"Come on nigga, I got a surprise for you." Making our way outside we got in the car and made our way to the back. Sparking up some dro we were in our own world until they knocked on the window. Getting in the car Quin turned and looked and smiled at me. Starting the car, we were on our way. Going to the Baymont Inn we both got our rooms and dapped each other up.

"Aye bro be careful, and I will see you in the morning." Giving him a pound me and chocolate went to our room.

Quin

Walking into the hotel room I couldn't believe I was in here with another woman. This bitch was bad though. "Hey Ms. Kitty come sit beside me." She pranced her ass by me and sat down.

"Damn, I thought you was going to smell like fish like the rest of them. You smell fruity and shit tho." I leaned over and smelled her looking like a creep.

"So what nigga you called me over here to insult me and smell me at the same time. Just because I shake my ass for a living don't mean I have to smell like those musty thots."

"You got that lil ma." She reached over me and started playing with my dick. Before I knew it, she had my dick hitting the back of her tonsils. This bitch could suck a golf ball through threw a straw. She had a nigga eyes rolling in the back of her head. Grabbing the back of her head I started to fuck her fast and hard. She had no gag reflex. Seeing the spit slip out her mouth had my man growing harder.

"THAT'S JUST THE WAY I LIKE IT. MAKE THAT SHIT SLOPPY." I reached down and slapped her ass making it jiggle. Emptying my seeds down her throat she didn't stop sucking. Making me hard once again. Hearing my phone vibrate in my pocket I didn't even care at that moment she had me feeling good. Standing her up I put that arch in her back and dived right in making my dick touch every part of her insides. She was tight as hell and was gripping my dick something serious. I had to think of panda bears and shit to keep me from busting again. Slapping her as with one hand and grabbing he hair with the next I was fucking her rough and hard. This bitch was going to remember my name. Flipping her over, I raised one leg back by her head and held the other one down. This bitch was flexible as hell. She was juicy as hell. Had my dick glistening. Watching her fuck faces she started to play with her clit while I rotated my dick inside of her. Touching her G-spot making her squirt. I pulled out and busted all over stomach. I had to get my composure together.

Walking out the room to the bathroom I turned the shower on and let the water massage me. Feeling a cold draft, she entered the bathroom with me, and we started round two. We didn't go to sleep until like seven in the morning.

Waking up, she was still sleep, so I wrote my number down and told her to hit me later. I needed that pussy again. Grabbing my phone, I text Prince and told him to meet me downstairs. Seeing him get off the elevator we made our way to the car and proceeded to King house to get dressed for the day. Looking at my phone I immediately had a wave of regret. I just cheated on the person who means the world to me. I know we was having our problems, but I didn't have to do her like that. I didn't even ware a fucking condom. I'm fucking up. Before I knew it, we were pulling up to Kings house. Stepping foot in the door Qua and King was sitting in the living room playing the game.

"Where the fuck y'all lil niggas been?" Qua asked us.

"Out getting pussy." Prince said smiling like a damn cheetah cat

"Man tell me you didn't do what I think you did nigga?" Qua stood up and made his way to me. I couldn't do nothing but hang my head low.

"Yo stupid ass cheated on Trinity. Do you know that girl is a certified killer? I am not trying to lose a brother and now yo dumb ass than put me in the middle. You fucking up homie and I be damn if you fuck up my shit with Serenity. You better dead that shit before sis finds out forreal. Twins or not I'm not going for that cheating bullshit and I am not covering for your ass. Serenity knows when I am lying to her. She gone feel some type of way. You better hope they don't both put that lead in your ass." He left out the living room and walked upstairs. He wasn't speaking nothing but facts. My bro haven't ever been disappointed in me and I can tell he bout to stress out now. Walking upstairs I grabbed my cloths and made my way to the shower a nigga needed to sleep but before sleep I needed to text my better half.

Me: Baby I know we don't see eye to eye right now. I know you pissed at a nigga but remember I love your ugly ass. Be safe and I will be back before you know it.

Seeing she read it because she had a nigga on read, I was happy even though she didn't reply back. I was just happy I wasn't blocked. Before my eyes closed, I saw a text.

Unknown: That dick was everything. I can't wait to taste you again (heart emoji)

Awwwww Fuck I just messed up.

Trinity

"Baby Quin please stop crying." Patting my son on his back I cuddled him against my breast. I didn't know what was wrong with my son, but he was not fucking with me today.

"Give him here sis." Sincere came into the room and took Quin Jr. out my hands. "Go lay down sis, I'm going to take him with me today." Seeing my son instantly stop crying when Sincere picked him up, I started crying. I didn't know if it was my hormones or if I was really hurt. My son or my man wasn't fucking with me. Rubbing my stomach, I walked into the bathroom and got in the shower. When I heard my door shut, I set in the shower and broke down. My stomach was hurting so I knew I was upsetting my baby, but I didn't know what to do but cry. Stepping out the shower I grabbed my phone and texted Serenity.

Me: I need you sis.

Sis: Sincere already told me. He's on his way to get the boys and I'm going to be on my way to you.

I didn't even text her back I just put on a big shirt and laid in my bed. I didn't even know I drifted off to sleep until I looked over and seen Serenity sleep besides me. I cuddle against my best friend and cried my eyes out. I guess she felt me crying because she started rubbing my hair.

"What's wrong Trinity, talk to me."

"I don't know sis. I don't fucking know. I'm losing it and I don't know why."

"Tell me what I can do to make you happy again."

"I need Quin. Please just get me Quin." I broke down while she reached for her phone and put it on speaker.

"Bae, can you please get Quin here. Trinity having a nervous breakdown and I don't know what to do." Serenity was now crying because I was crying.

"We on our way. Calm down ma and try to calm her down before she hurts my niece. I love you."

"I-I- lo-ve yo-u to." Hanging up she pulled me into her and cried with me. This was a true fucking best friend. She was really hurting with me and I couldn't even tell her why I was hurting hell I didn't even know why I was hurting. Eventually I fell to sleep and when I woke up it was nighttime. Putting on my robe I found Serenity and Sincere sitting in the living room with the babies laying on the floor sleep. When they seen me they looked at me with sympathy. Sincere got up and came to hug me. Even though this was my best friend little brother he was my little brother to. When he hugged me, it felt like all my problems went away for the time being.

"I don't know what's going on, but I love you Trinity. When you need me I'll come running." Kissing my check, he went and grabbed me a water from the fridge. Laying on the couch I placed my head in Serenity lap and she leaned down and kissed my forehead.

"Bae where you at." Quin came flying through the door with a worried Qua behind him. Hoping up I jumped in his arms and cried. "Ma you gotta talk to me. What's wrong."

"I don't know, I'm just so tired. Baby Quin been crying since you left, I haven't gotten any sleep. This is why I didn't want you to leave this pregnancy is draining me I don't feel like myself." Breaking down in his arms, I pulled him to the ground with me.

"Sis, it's gone be okay." Qua leaned down and pulled me out of Quins arms and hugged me tight. I had so much support, but I felt so alone. "Let's give them some space ma." Grabbing their boys Serenity and Qua gave me one last hug before they walked out the door to go home while Sincere took Quin Jr, to his room.

"Alright y'all imma head out. Trinity, I meant what I said call me if you need me." Kissing me on the forehead and dapping up Quin, Sincere walked out the house and Quin carried me to the room.

Serenity

Man I never seen my bestfriend so broken like that. I'm used to that 'bitch you will get cut Trinity, that shit talking trinity, and that bitch you ridin or naw Trinity.' Seeing her like this put her in perspective that at any time you can break. I didn't know what to do besides sit with her and cry. I'm glad Sincere came and got the baby because she was losing her mind even more.

Looking over at my future husband I couldn't wait to marry him. We had exactly 4 months until I was Mrs. Quadir Richardson. Grabbing his hand, I held it until we were almost home. My two blessings were in the back and I was riding side by side with my man.

"Bae is everything ok with Quin. He looked a little off today when he came in?"

"He cool bae, they just going through some things. He was hurt when Trin basically told him he was a dead-beat father. To us being a father is everything. Our father was in our life all the time. He taught us the game, but not just that he taught us sports. He taught us the birds and bees, but most importantly he taught us to know when we picked a great woman." He looked at me and I saw the smile and happiness through his eyes. I wanted to reach over, pull that dick out and suck the shit out of it. My kitty in dire need of some loving and stroking.

Pulling up to the house it was late at night, so we had to get the twins situated. Giving them their baths, we put them in the beds and turned the monitor on. Grabbing my, rob I made it to the bathroom and turned on all shower heads. We had the best shower ever. Water hit you from all sides. The pressure was awesome, and it felt like a mini orgasm. Standing directly in the middle I felt a draft of cold air. I already knew what was happening. Bending over I gave him all access to my kitty. Grabbing one leg he penetrated me deeply and making sure to make her purrrr.

"Damn bae, you were ready huh?"

"Oooo, yassssss, daddy, hit that pussy, right there, smack that ass……..oooooo shit BAEEEEEE." Yelling I was hoping the twins stayed sleep. He had me bent like a pretzel making a bitch talk in tongue." Cumming together we washed up and got out the shower. Lying in bed I had him binge watching All American, this was my show and he was fineeeeee. I'm glad he was legally of age or I would feel like a pedophile. Seeing that Qua feel asleep, I turned the TV off and joined my bae.

Waking up the next morning Qua was not in the bed with me. I checked my phone and sent Trinity a text telling her to get some rest me and Qua will handle everything today. Today was the day that we were meeting with the chefs to see which one we wanted for the soul food restaurant. We needed to have one main chef and we would let him pick his prodigy. Handling my hygiene and getting dressed I walked out the room to the twin's room. Qua was in there fighting trying to get them together.

"Need some help daddy?"

"Hell yes, these lil niggas have they own mind. I believe they ass in cahoots with each other. I get one dressed. Then the other one wants to start trying to crawl. Baby I solute you, you the real MVP." I walked over to him and grabbed the baby while he kissed my cheek. Grabbing baby Qua I kissed all over his handsome chocolate face. He was damn near dressed so while we tag-teamed they lil asses and was on our way. Thank God that Qua was fully dressed, or it would have been a lot longer.

Pulling up to the restaurant we got the children out and made it to the office. It was a long line outside waiting to get the chef spot. After three hours of interviewing we had our chef. He was excited and I knew he would bring us in a lot of revenue. Even though Qua wasn't with these opportunities at first, he seems more involved. He was loving being a family man and becoming legit.

Trinity

"Hey baby you feeling better?" Quin asked me as I walked down the stairs. Last night was a world wind of events. I never broke down like that before. This shit was crazy. I didn't know if I was coming or going, but I thank God for my sis and brother.

"I am feeling a lil better. Can you go get us something to eat? I don't want to cook."

"Yes baby, what you want?"

"I want some rib tips, with sweet potatoes, and greens, oooooo and some red velvet cake. Make sure it has a lot of icing."

"Alright I got you." Standing up. He grabbed his keys before heading out the door.

DING

Looking over at the table I seen that Quin left his phone and it was blowing up. Picking it up it said that somebody name Kevin was calling him. Answering it, a female voice came through the phone.

"Hey baby, I miss you." I know I had to be losing my fucking mind. I know a bitch was not on the other side of this fucking phone.

"Who the fuck is this." I now had tears falling down my face.

"I'm sorry is this Quin's phone."

"Yes, it is, who the fuck are you I'm not gone ask you again." *Click!* This bitch hung up on me. Putting Quin's passcode in I went to the messages.

Kevin: I miss you when can I have that dick again

Quin: I'll see you when I come back to flint ma

Kevin: lol okay, are you going to facetime me tonight

Quin: I have a business meeting I have to go to tonight

Kevin: I haven't been able to see yo face in a couple days

Quin: I know ma I'm going to change it.

Kevin: (*Picture message*)

This bitch had the nerve to be pretty to. With tears still coming down my face I continued to read the messages. Lunging his phone at the wall I threw on my robe and went straight to his closet. Grabbing his clothes out I went straight to the bathroom and started pouring bleach on them. I know I probably looked like a crazy woman with my robe all open and my lingerie on. I had my recently installed thirty-inch hair curled to perfection hanging down my back and my mascara was running down my face with my tears.

"Ouch." When I felt my baby kick, I knew I had to do something different then pour bleach on his clothes because I was harming my child. Picking up some more of his clothes I walked outside and started throwing his clothes out the window.

"Two babies later and this nigga want to cheat on me." Taking the TV, I knocked the bitch off the wall than used a bat to smash the first picture that me and him took that was hanging on the wall. Falling to the floor in glass all I let out a gut-wrenching cry.

"Bae, I left my phone up here have you seen it." Looking up at Quin he looked guilty as fuck.

"Why, why was I not good enough for you." I didn't even have the energy to scream. "I thought I was a good woman Quincy, I take care of you and our kids and you go out and cheat on me. What did I do to make you do me like this?" Walking over to me he got on his knees and pulled me into him. "DON'T FUCKING TOUCH ME. ANSWER ME NIGGA, ANSWER ME NOW."

"I fucked up bae." This nigga had the nerves to have tears coming down his face. "Please don't leave."

"AHHHHHHHHHHHH, why Quin why would you do this to us. We wasn't perfect but damn we a fucking family. I want you out my fucking house." Balling my fist up I punched him dead in his eye hoping that bitch blacked. Grabbing me up off the ground he slammed me into the wall but then let me go when I grabbed my belly.

"I don't put my hands on you so don't put yo fucking hands on me. I said I fucked up, I cheated but I can't take that shit back. That little striper bitch don't mean shit to me. The shit happened when I went to flint and me and you were into it when you tried to make me feel like less than a fucking father." The audacity of this nigga, I know he wasn't trying to make this shit seem like it was my fault.

"No, No. No you can't blame me for your fuck up muthafucka. I want you out my fucking house NOW."

"I'm not go-"

"Please quin just leave. You lucky my baby in the house or else this bitch would have been burned to the fucking ground. NOW GET THE FUCK OUT."

"I'm going to leave so you can calm down but this conversation ain't over." He started walking out the door.

"As far as I'm concerned not only is this conversation over but so is this relationship. Bye Quin." He stopped but then walked out our room door. Watching him walk out the door was the hardest thing I ever did. I waited until I heard our alarm system before I went to check on my son, when I seen that he slept through it all I went to the guest bathroom and took a shower. Stepping under the hot water I broke down. How could Quin do this to me, our first argument and he goes and sleep with a stripper. A fucking stripper. I don't know how I was about to get through this but I had to. As much as I loved him, I couldn't be with him. I couldn't be with a cheating ass nigga. After washing up I got out the shower and put on some pjs. Grabbing my son out his crib I cuddled with him in the guest bedroom until I cried myself to sleep. Fuck my life.

Quin

Man fuck I done messed up. I just got put out the house that I pay the bills for. Granted a nigga just fucked up. I didn't love that hoe, but she did give some fire ass sloppy toppy. Now I'm out here ass out and done fucked up and possibly lost my family. My family was my life.

Driving around my city, I had to be by myself. My phone just kept ringing, so I turned it off it was only Qua calling. Guaranteed Trinity done called Serenity and now Qua knew. I didn't want to hear that 'told you so' shit. I knew I had some ass kissing to do. Shit I might have to eat the booty.

Pulling up to the gym, I had to release some anger. This gym was a gym and gun range all in one that my pops owned. Putting on my boxing gloves I started punching the bag. I started to think about the first time I invited Trinity to my house and when I admitted to falling in love with her.

"You got a nice ass house, you gone give me a tour." She was running her hands along my marble island that I had in the middle of the kitchen.

"Yeah let's go tour the master bedroom real quick."

"Nigga no. I want a tour of everything but yo master bedroom."

"Come on ugly ass girl." Shaking her head, she followed me through the house. She was impressed as fuck especially when she got to the indoor pool with the jacuzzi next to it.

"I can't wait to go swimming in this. Can you swim?"

"I'm grown as fuck, why wouldn't I be able to swim? Can you Swim?"

"Yes, me and Serenity was on our high school swimming team." She smiled bright as fuck and I had to smile seeing her smile.

"Yo, y'all white as fuck man."

"Whatever, can we freshen up and go watch tv in your theater room." She walked up to me and put her hands around my neck.

"It's yo world I'm just living in it baby." Kissing her cheek, I lead her to the guest bedroom and showed her where all the stuff was for her shower.

"I'm right across the hall from you if you need me. Nodding her head, she disappeared in the bathroom.

This shower didn't do nothing for the hardon I had from just being around Trinity. This girl was getting under my skin and making her black ass into my heart and I didn't know how to feel about that. I never been in love before, but damn I felt like this is what it felt like. Just being around short gave me piece and I needed that with the world I lived in. Letting the shower run over my waves, I thought about me life. I was a successful black criminal and every woman I ever came in contact with wanted me for my name and my money. So, being around a woman with her own money and who didn't give a damn about mines was foreign to me. After handling my hygiene, I slipped on some grey sweats and with no shirt on and made my way back across the hall. Without even knocking I walked in the room and got a eye full.

"Damn." I whispered to myself more than her. She was looking in the mirror staring at her damn near perfect body and we locked eyes in the mirror. I was stuck looking at shorty because her body was banging and it was all fucking natural.

"So, I just remembered, I don't have any clothes here. Can you bring me a shirt?" My words were caught in my throat so I nodded and headed back to my room to get her a shirt.

"Here ma." I handed her the shirt and watched her bring it over her body. I had to smirk when my shirt followed her whole.

"Oh, he can talk again." She giggled, and I almost passed out. What the fuck was this girl doing to me.

"Come on man, let's go watch some movies. What you want to watch?"

"Bluehill Avenue." I had to do a doubletake and look at here because I didn't think I heard her right.

"What, just cause I'm cute don't mean I don't watch hood shit. Tristian the truth baby."

"This shit is crazy, that's me and Twin favorite movie."

"Yeah, it is crazy because that's me and Serenity favorite movie to. I guess it was meant to be." I don't know how we made it to the bed, but I remembered sleeping with her in my arms. When I woke up she wasn't there anymore, so I followed the sound of her music and found her in the pool doing laps. She did about three laps before she noticed me sitting in the chair next to the pool. Smiling she swim to where I was.

"Good morning. Get in." He hair was wet and dripping over her face. That shit made her even more beautiful.

"Let me get my trunks." Standing up I stretched.

"Don't bother, I don't have one on either." With that she slipped back under the water and started swimming again. Taking off my sweats, I dived in the water and took off swimming after her. This was life man, I could see myself with this woman for the long run. After a hour of swimming and playing in the pool, we ended up in the jacuzzi with me sitting between her legs and her rubbing my head.

"What's yo plan for life." She asked, and I thought before I answered.

"To be honest, I always thought I's be a drug dealer my whole life. I never thought about having a wife or any kids. I always planned on being by myself and getting this money." Taking a breath, I begin talking again.

"Then I met yo ugly ass." Slapping my arm, she smiled, and I continued. "You make me feel

complete, like you my peace and that's all a nigga need. I never felt what I feel about you and I if I didn't know any better I'd think I'm falling for you." Sitting up, I pulled her on top of me and she straddled me.

"I'm glad you said that, cause I'm falling for you to." Kissing her I tapped her ass and she got up.

"Let's get out of here before I have yo chocolate ass bent over in this jacuzzi."

"You know how to ruin the moment, huh." Wrapping a towel around herself she switched back to the room, but not before turning around and smiling at me. "In case you didn't know, you're mines." Winking at me she smiled again and walked away.

I punched the bag until it was on the fucking floor with tears rolling down my face, until I felt somebody bear hug me and stop me from falling. I knew from the connection that it was my brother, him and my pops the only people who knew this was my get away spot.

"I'm good Qua. I'm good." Taking the boxing gloves off I walked to the back where the gun range was at and Qua followed suit. Picking up our guns we started aiming and shooting without saying another word. I didn't even realize Qua was done shooting until I looked by my side and he wasn't there.

"You good, you ready to talk now."
"I fucked up bro, that bitch wasn't worth losing my family. When Trinity told me, she was done with our relationship, I wanted to turn

around and fucking strangle her. It took everything in my power not to smack fire out her ass when she blacked my fucking eye. Do you see this shit?" Pointing at my eye Qua just shook his head.

"I'm bouta give it to you raw no lube bro. Wait that shit just sounded so fucking gay." I looked at him and we both laughed till tears fell from our eyes. Leave up to my brother to say some dumb shit when I'm pissed off. "Naw, for real though bro, you fucked up. You shouldn't have stayed at that strip club with Prince young ass. You know that nigga wild as fuck and single, he don't answer to nobody, that's why he didn't give a fuck. You on the other hand, you knew better. You knew better than to bring that stripper bitch to the room with you. You knew better than to break Trinity heart the way you did. When she called Serenity, she sounded like she could barely fucking breath. She's hurting bro. The mother of your children, the woman that hold the key to yo fucking heart is broken cause you couldn't keep yo dick in yo pants. Bro you fucking folded on your woman and possibly lost her because you couldn't handle a little fucking argument. You know she didn't mean shit that she said. But trust me when I say, if Serenity don't get in Trinity ass for the way she talked to you I am because all of this not on you. Yeah you fucked up, but she fucked up to. Pick yo fucking head up and go get yo woman." Pausing he looked at me. "Never mind she crazy as fuck don't talk to her right now." Chuckling I looked at my bro and he looked at me like I was crazy.

"Qua bro, you don't even understand how scary her ass looked when she was staring at me. She had on her robe with some lingerie on and her stomach was poking through it. She had her hair curled and shit, but her eyes was black. When I walked through the door the whole fucking tv in our room was in pieces on the floor and it smelled like straight bleach.

On the low she had my thug as scared, I thought it was over for me." I shook my head as Qua was on the ground crying laughing. His ass was laughing at my pain and I couldn't do nothing but chuckle with him.

"By the way, moms and pops said come by the house." If y'all thought Trinity had me scared, my mom's was ten times worst. *Fuck my life.*

Serenity

"Damn bestie, I'm sorry you have to go through this. You don't deserve what is happening to you. But I'm about to spit some straight 'G' shit to you. Quin, yea he did some foul shit. It makes me want to throat punch his ass. Trinity but you, you bruised that man ego. You told him he basically wasn't shit and he wasn't a good dad. He been there for you since the day y'all met. Y'all have this undeniable bond. The love y'all have for one another is that one in a million love. He been there for Quin Jr. that little boy loves his daddy. You need to be the woman I taught you to be. Put your big girl panties on and face the music. Get your man back. Make him pay yes, but, let him know this will be the last time. Next time he won't be breathing."

"Bitch you tried it, ha, you taught me. Naw daddy taught us this shit. I feel you though sis. I didn't mean for it to get this far. You know I'm spoiled and feel everything need to go on my terms. I'm hormonal and just waiting for this lil girl to give me my space back. I'm going to get my man back but first we bout to tell this lady to come back so we can get this fitting done for this dress."

Watching the alteration lady come back out she led me back to my room. Seeing my dress hanging on the door made me emotional. I am really getting married in 2 weeks. Stepping into my dress. It fit me like a glove, it wasn't too tight but it gave the princess and sexy feeling. I already had my shoes, so I put them on along with my vail. Stepping out the door Trinity was sitting there scrolling through her phone.

"You like it." I asked her with tears in my eyes.

"AHHHH YASSSSS BITCH YASSSSS YOU DID THAT." Crying she wobbled to me hugging and kissing me on the face."

"I wish daddy was here."

"No not today. I'm not for that today. I got you sis. Sincere got you the locket so in a way he will be walking you down the aisle with our daddy."

After I dropped Trinity off at home, I made my way home hoping that my man was already at home waiting for me. Walking through the front door I dropped my keys on the front table and slipped my shoes off my feet. Following the smell of weed I made my way into my husband office.

"What's up ma." Walking over to the couch in his office I laid out on the couch.

"What's wrong bae. You look stressed as fuck." Lifting his head up I slid under him and laid his head in my lap.

"I'm worried about my fucking brother man. You know his ass didn't show up for the fucking suit fitting. I'm pissed off because how the fuck am I supposed to marry the love of my fucking life without my twin standing right beside me."

"See, yeah no. We not about to go through this. Come on." Pushing his head out my lap I stood up. I'd be damned if Quin ass fucked up my wedding.

"Ahh bae, what the fuck."

"We going to get his ass."

Walking out the house I was glad the kids was with ma and pops. We jumped into the car and made our way to the hotel that Quin was staying. Having Qua play that he was Quin we were able to get the keycard without Quin knowing. Taking the elevator to the top floor. I knew this nigga had nothing but the best. Swiping the card, we walked into Quin playing Toni Braxton, Unbreak My heart, with nothing but his underwear on drinking Hennessey with no chaser.

"Don't leave me in all this pain, Don't leave me out in the rain, Come back and bring back my smile, Come and take these tears away, I need your arms to hold me now, The nights are so unkind, Bring back those nights when I held you beside me, Un-break my heart, Say you'll love me again, Undo this hurt you caused, When you walked out the door, And walked out of my life, Un-cry these tears, I cried so many nights, Un-break my heart, My heart"

"Naw bro, we not going out like that." I walked over to the lights and turned them on. Turning down the music I went to start the shower while Qua was in the room talking to him. I never seen my bro like this.

Him and Trinity is going through it. They so much alike that it was scary. Coming out the room, Qua was guiding him in the bathroom.

Hearing the shower cut off, I sat down in the living area and waited for him to come out. "Quin, I need for you to get it together. What's this I hear about you missing the final fitting for your tux. Now I don't want you to be saying that this shit doesn't fit, because you will be the only motherfucker up there that's fucked up, now play with me."

"Damn sis. I did forget but I have a lot on my mind. I need my baby back. It's like I can't function without her."

"I know, but you sitting in this hotel not going to get her back. Take yo ass home, sleep in the guess room, nigga I don't care. You need to show her that you at least trying. Don't leave tonight because you drunk and y'all might get into it, but tomorrow get your shit together. I will call the people and have them get you in at 3 o'clock. You better not forget or I'm going to turn into bridezilla on yo ass. Now play with me." Kissing his cheek, I grabbed Qua's hand and led him out the door as he dapped Quin up.

"Baby, you served his ass. Got my dick hard and shit," Hearing that I dragged his ass to the car so we can head home and fuck like rabbits.

Quin

Waking up this morning I had a massive migraine, but I needed to do what sis said. Grabbing my shit, I got dressed and checked out the hotel. Going to my car I put back on Toni Braxton. She helped me through this shit right now. Pulling up to the house I used the garage door opener to get in. I am surprised that she didn't change the locks me. Turning the alarm off. I reset it again once I had the doors locked. Taking my shoes off I went straight to my son room and grabbed him out his crib. Laying him on my chest. I looked at him while he slept. Yeah, I had to get my family back.

"Daddy sorry little man I messed up bad and I haven't been here for you and your mama. I did some messed up shit. I promise to be a better father to you and teach you all the stuff that my father taught me." Kissing the top of his head I laid my head back and closed my eyes.

Hearing Trinity, my eyes shot open and I realized my baby was back in his crib. Trinity was looking at me and I didn't know what to say. Standing up I tried to hug her but she moved back.

"What you doing here?" Her voice sounded so cold it sent a shiver down my spine.

"Trinity, ma we have to fix this. If I have to beg and plead with you for all eternity, I want my family back."

"You wasn't thinking about that in Flint. You weren't thinking about me." By then tears was streaming down her beautiful face."

"I'm sorry ma, I won't sleep in the room with you. I will be staying in the house, but I will be in the guest room. I need to be around my son and feel the presence of my woman even if she don't want me around at the moment." Looking at me she rolled her eyes and walked out the room.

Going to grab my stuff out of our room, I moved it to the guest room that was close to my son. Jumping in the shower again, I let the water run over my head while my thoughts clouded my mind. I still couldn't believe I broke the only woman heart that mattered. Trinity, my whole fucking world and seeing her all broken was fucking with me. After my 45-minute shower I laid back on the bed before it was time for me to go get fitted for my tux. I didn't even realize I had fell to sleep until my I heard my phone ringing.

"Nigga, don't forget about yo tux fitting, I'm meeting yo ass up there."

"I got you bruh, I'm about to leave out the house now. Do me a favor swing by the gas station and grab me a Red bull and some BC powder. I'm not gone have time to do that."

"I got you bruh. See you in a bit." Walking out the room I was passing by me and Trinity room and overheard her and Serenity conversation since she had her on speakerphone. Leaning against the wall by the door, I listened to it because it sounded like my woman was crying.

"Serenity, I'm so fucking mad at him but when I seen him with Jr on his chest I wanted to fuck and punch him at the same time. Why did he do this to us sis. How could he hurt me like this? To make things worst baby girl feel his presence and she fucking me up, doing flips and kicking my ass. I want him to stay away from me, but I want his fine ass to come in here and rub on my belly to."

"Trinity, if you don't go in there and get yo man back, you know I walked in on that nigga singing unbreak my heart by Toni Braxton. Sis, my bro hurting just like you maybe a little more." I couldn't stay to hear the rest of the conversation but now that I knew that Trinity didn't really want to leave me, I knew what I had to do next.

Walking to my charger I jumped in, waited for my phone to connect to the Bluetooth and took off towards the tux place. Qua black charger was the first thing I noticed, and I shook my head, not only did me and this nigga have the same face but we thought alike to. I hated and loved that shit at the same time.

"When I got out my car a group of girls was walking out the place." I smirked at the little comments that they were saying. Walking to Qua car he got out and dapped me up, handing me the Red bull and BC pack.

"Damn, it's two of y'all I promise I would fuck the shit out of both of y'all together." This fine ass redbone said and me and Qua, smirking and shaking our heads we walked into the building.

"Just think about it bro, two years ago we would have fucked that bitch together." Qua ass was right, we fucked plenty of bitches together in our younger days.

"Hell yeah, I'm not looking at another bitch, my woman already hot with my ass. I'm not tryna make Trinity kill my black ass. Not only Trinity, but yo short feisty ass wife to."

"Quadir, welcome back. Is this the last person who has to get fitted?" Some ugly ass old lady came to me and grabbed my hand and pulled me to the back. This lady was not playing no fucking games. She took my measurements, I tried on my suit and was out of the building within a couple of minutes.

After all was said and done, I stopped at this dog breeder house and picked up a pretty ass Pitbull puppy. I would have gotten the yorkie, but Trinity ass was a savage and probably would have killed that poor thing. Grabbing a bow for the dog, some flowers, some chocolate, and a card from Walgreens, I headed home to Trinity.

The first thing I heard when I walked into the house was Monica Why her. I hated that I made my baby feel like she wasn't enough. I set the dog down and her playful ass run right up to Trinity rubbing against her.

"What the hell?" She damn near jumped out of her skin before she bent down and picked up the dog. "Who is this little doggy?"

"She's yours, I mean she might be Jr's a little more but that's the new addition to the family.

"A dog won't make it work Quin, I just need some space." Trinity started crying again and grabbed her stomach. Walking up to her I hugged her from behind while rubbing her belly. Leaning against me, I felt her relax a little before snatching away from me and walking to the other room. Looking at Jr, I picked him up and took him to the bathroom to get him cleaned up. I had a lot of fucking ass kissing to do.

2 weeks later Serenity

Rehearsal dinner

"I'm not walking down the aisle with him Serenity and that's final. You already getting married while I'm eight months pregnant you, betta be lucky that I'm even walking my fat ass down this aisle tomorrow." Trinity set on the couch in the bathroom with tears falling down her eyes.

"Trinity please don't do this to me. Please don't do this before my wedding." I was pacing back and forth with tears in my eyes.

"Serenity, you know me and him not on good terms, I don't want to walk with him, talk to him, I don't even want to be in the same room as him. Hell, you already told him to move back into the house with me."

"DAMN IT TRINITY, DO IT FOR ME. PLEASE DON'T DO THIS TO ME." I broke down crying.

"Okay, for you. I will do it for you. But I promise you, you fucking owe me." She walked over to the bathroom sink and wet a paper towel and came to hand it to me. "Get yo cry baby ass off this nasty ass floor." Laughing I got off the floor and wiped my face, just as there was a knock at the door.

"Serenity and Trinity what the fuck are y'all doing. People out here waiting on y'all." Qua's deep as voice boomed through the bathroom door.

"Here we come bae." Serenity walked out the door and kissed Qua on the lips. "We had to have a little talk."

"You good sis?" Qua came and hugged Trinity.

"As good as I'm going to be." Qua knew Trinity wasn't fucking with him really so he let her go and walked back to the room.

"Yo ass mean as fuck." I nudged Trin and we walked back to the area where everybody was waiting to start the rehearsal.

"No, sis I'm angry and hurt as fuck. It's a difference." As soon as we walked into the area where everyone else was at Quin stood up and stood next to his brother. It looked like Quin was tired and Jr was tired. I hoped like hell they got it together for their children sack because this was some bullshit. My niece and nephew was not about to grow up in a broken home. After the Rehearsal dinner Qua went with Quin and I went with Trinity.

Sitting on the couch in the hotel suite we had, me, Trinity, Kenzie and Sapphire was drinking some red wine.

"So, no for real, how it feels to be with King fine ass." As soon as Sapphire said that Kenzie looked at her like she done lost her fucking mind.

"Nu un boo, you betta stop playing before yo fine ass be coming home with me. Me and my man love strippers." Kenzie blew Sapphire a kiss. Sapphire crazy ass got up and started twerking with her Cranberry juice in one hand and her other hand in the air.

"Naw, you stop playing with me because I fuck bitches to, Pregnant and all boo I'll be in y'all room with y'all." Sapphire winked at Kenzie. We were having so much fun until there was a knock at the door. As soon as I opened the door, Qua, Quin, King and Prince drunk asses came into the room with two bottles of Black Henny a piece. Grabbing me in his arm Qua tongued me down so good that I got weak in the knees.

"Bae, I wasn't supposed to see you until tomorrow." Pulling me into the room that I was in. He laid me on the bed and kissed my neck.

"I know ma, but I'm drunk as fuck and I needed my wife. You ready to officially be Mrs. Quadir Richardson. "Placing kisses down my stomach he licked around my belly button.

"ohhhh shit bae, I was ready, fuck right there." I couldn't even finish talking because he kept flicking his tongue around my pearl.

"Talk to me ma, you ready to become Mrs. Quadir Richardson." His voice was muffled cause he had a mouth full right me.

"Yes daddy, I'm ready to become Mrs. Quadir Richardson. Ahhhhhh fuck." I started cumming all in his mouth trying to pull away from him. Placing his hand on my stomach he kept me in place and kept sucking my soul out of me. "baeeeeeeee, please."

"Please what, it's mines right." Nodding my head because I couldn't talk, he smirked at me. "Well let me eat in piece then ma, a nigga hungry." Placing my hands on his head I let my man bring me another orgasm before I got away from his ass. Fucking around with him he was gone eat me to death before I even became his Mrs. Jumping off the bed, I pushed him on the bed and straddled him. Looking down at him I couldn't help but smile at my soon to be husband.

"Your so fucking beautiful daddy." His smile instantly dropped when I said that and I laughed.

"You so fucking gay man. Get the fuck off me." Tracing the tattoos on his chest I placed kisses on them afterwards. "What you gone do with that?" He placed me on his growing dick and I instantly hopped up and he helped me help him take off the True Religion Jeans he had on. My mouth started to water as soon as we got them off. Taking my tongue, I licked around the head and looked him in the eyes just before his head fell back. Taking him in my mouth I deep throated him than started to suck it while doing the two-hand twister.

"Shit, ma." His breathing started picking up and I knew I was doing the damn thing. "Alright ma, fuck." Grabbing me up by the shoulders he tongued me down again. I don't know about y'all, but I loved for my nigga to tongue me down right after I sucked his dick. Me and my man was nasty like that. "Assume the Position." Laying on my stomach I tooted my ass up and my arch was perfect, looking back at him I reached behind me and put his tip at my opening right before he plunged into me.

"Ahhhhhhhhh." I started throwing my ass back at him and he was catching it.

"Hell yeah, ma throw that shit back. You gone cum on daddy dick." *slap slap slap* "Huh, you gone cum for me ma."

"Yesssss daddy, righttttt ouuuuu. Right there da- fuck daddyyyyyyyy." Pulling out he laid down and set me directly on his face and started sucking my clit with no mercy. Licking me dry, I fell into the headboard.

"Naw, wake that ass up get up here and milk me dry ma." I couldn't let him out fuck me, so I slid down on his dick and started riding him like I was in a rodeo. Spinning around with his dick still inside me, I gave him the perfect view of my ass. When I felt him throbbing inside me, I turned back around and started bouncing up and down on him with kissing him long deep and hard. Taking my hips, he started slamming me into him.

"Ahhhhhhh, cum with my ma. You gone come with daddy." Nodding my head, we both exploded together. Leaning against the headboard I fell against his chest as we both tried to catch our breath. "I love you mama."

"I love you to daddy, but we gotta go take a shower because we still got people out there." I laughed and climbed off him. After our shower we went back in the sitting area of the room. I wasn't surprised when I saw Sapphire, Kenzie and King deep in a conversation.

"Where's Trinity?"

"She in there sleep." Quin had a scowl on his face, so I knew they had to have gotten into it. "I'm about to head to the room, I'm drunk and tired as fuck." Dapping up everybody he walked out the room.

"Bae, did yo brother just dap me?" I doubled over in laughter. "I'm about to go check on Trinity, are you sleeping here with me tonight or going back to the room."

"Imma follow tradition a little ma." I helped Qua off the couch he was on and he put his hands around my waist.

"I'll see you tomorrow baby, I'll be the one in the big beautiful white dress."

"Okay ma, I'll be the one at the altar waiting for you." Kissing him on the lips he smiled down on me.

"Serenity, imma go to the room with Kenzie and King." Sapphire got off the couch and walked out the room followed by the couple. Shaking my head, I laughed at them and kissed my baby one more time before I went and climbed in bed with Trinity. It broke my heart when I heard her crying in her sleep and holding her belly.

"Is it bad that I still love him Serenity, it hurts so much." This whole time I thought she was sleep she was in here crying. Pulling her head against my boobs, I kissed her forehead.

"No, it's not crazy Trin. That's love and y'all gone get it together I promise you." I held her while she cried until we both went to sleep.

Sincere

The morning of the wedding

Waking up this morning I remembered my sis was getting married today. I was walking her down the aisle and giving her away to my nigga Qua. I must admit I never thought I would have seen her settle down. She was always on her shit and always said a 'nigga would only slow her down.' I had to hurry up and get dressed. She was waiting for me to pick her up.

Going to her room, I knocked on the door and she came out grabbing my hand.

"Good morning beautiful, you ready for today?"

"As ready as I ever will be."

We made it to the car, and I started driving to see our dad. This is something that she probably didn't want to do but it something that we both needed. "I am so happy I am giving you away today. You don't know what this means to me. If only daddy was here to see you now."

"I would have really like for my parents to have been there. Daddy will forever be with me but that bitch ass mother of ours I would have shot her in the face. Have you spoke to her lately?"

"Naw, I went by their house and the house was completely empty. I guess once they figured out, we were on to them they decided it was time for them to leave." I told her as we were going pulling up to our daddy grave site. Helping he out the car we went and set by our daddy grave.

"Hey daddy, your baby girl is getting married today. This day was envisioned by you walking me down the aisle in a big princess cut dress, but I have to settle on wearing you around my neck. Your baby girl has done so good for herself. Me and Trinity both have families even though she wants to kick her future husband ass right now. My twins, dad, you would have loved them. They remind me of you. they have their own personality, but they are a force to be reckoned with. I am going to make sure I tell them about their papa." By the time Serenity was done she was crying while I was hugging her.

This have been the hardest thing to do. I haven't been to my father grave in a very long time. "What's up pops? This is crazy the shit that I found out about ma is crazy. I wish I would have known what they were up to because I wouldn't have gone away. They did this to you and took you away from us. We needed you. if you wouldn't have installed in us what we know today then we would have been lost because this bitch just said fuck us with no lube. Dad I will protect both of my sisters and will continue to make you proud. I love you old man." Serenity and I kissed his headstone, and we were on our way.

"Sis I didn't mean to make you cry but we both needed that."

"I know bro. I will always love you."

Pulling back up to the hotel I helped her out and she went back to her room while I went to mines.

Qua

The wedding

"I'm so fucking proud of you bro." Quin and our pops stood in front of me helping me put on my tie on. Quin wiped the single tear that fell from my eye and pulled me into a brotherly hug.

"Thanks bro." Grabbing a pre-lit blunt we set back with the Royalty brothers and our pops. Our pops even sparked one with us today.

"You almost on my side bro." King dapped me up handing me a watch. "I consider you a brother, so this is my gift to you." He handed me a all gold Rolex and I had to admit that bitch was nice.

"Thanks bro."

"Qua let me talk to you real quick." Pulling me out the room, Quin handed me a ring box.

"What's this." Opening the box, I closed it back cause that bitch almost blinded me. "You want to propose to Trinity at the reception?"

"If it's okay with you. I already talked to Serenity and she's okay with it."

"Do yo thing bro, I'm ready for y'all to get y'all shit together."

"Good looking." Walking back into the room we ran right into our mother. "You look so fucking beautiful ma." Quin kissed her on the cheek, and I kissed the other side.

"I do what I can do." She smiled at us. "Qua, I want you to know how proud I am of you. I never seen myself attending neither of your weddings but Babyboy you proved me wrong. You proved to me that you didn't want to be a hoe your whole life." She took my hand into hers. "Do right by her Qua. Now they ready downstairs, so let's go get you married." Wiping the tears from her eyes I walked with my mama, my best man, dad and my groomsmen behind me. I was really about to get fucking married.

Standing at the alter I watched as all our wedding party was walking down the aisle. I couldn't help but fucking notice how nice my bro and Trinity looked. My mind cleared when I heard John Legend *All of me start playing*. My baby was getting ready to grace our presence, when everyone stood up the doors opened and Serenity and Sincere started walking out.

my head's under water but I'm breathing fine you're crazy and I'm out of my mind 'cause all of me loves all of you love your curves and all your edges all your perfect imperfections give your all to me I'll give my all to you you're my end and my beginning even when I lose I'm winning 'cause I give you all, all of me and you give me all

Watching my wife walk down the aisles was enough to make any nigga want to fall down to his knees. When she made it to me and it was time for Sincere to give her away, he hugged her and came to stand by us. The pastor stood at the alter and I barely heard anything he said until "Quadir and Serenity wrote their own vows." Snapping out of looking at Serenity beautiful face.

"Qua, my love, my heartbeat, my man and my best friend. I never knew I would love someone as much as I love you. I came into this relationship a ghetto girl, but you help make me into the woman I am today. You loved me beyond the hurt, the pain, the foolishness and when I tried to leave you, you brought me back to you. You helped me make two bad sons. The thug I met before became the man I see today. I can't wait to see you old, I can't wait to spend the rest of eternity to with you."

When she was finished there wasn't a dry eye in the room. I had to top that.

"Serenity, baby, I cant…..Naw I'm just playing. Baby I love you so much. You are my rock, my piece, my everything. When I'm feeling down you lift me back up. You give me the love and attention that you know I can't live without. You have a heart of gold to deal with me and my mini me's. I remember when I first saw you in that club. You played me, in my mind I was already picturing you with my last name. We fit together; we finish each other sentences. We have that one and a lifetime love and baby with you by my side I will continue to grow and be the man that you need me to be. I will be your support, I will be your friend, I will kiss your tears away but most of all I will be YOUR HUSBAD."

Finishing up our vows. We kissed long and deep. We were finally married. I couldn't wait to put more babies in her. Jumping the broom, the wedding party made our way out the building.

After taking the pictures it was time to party.

"LET'S INTRODUCE THE KING AND QUEEN. HUSBAND AND WIFE MR AND MRS QUADIR RICHARDSON." The DJ announced us as we came in the ball room. This room was filled with the best. Our cake was five tiers high. With the letter R and a bride and groom."

"Hey Mrs. Richardson, can I have this dance." Taking serenity hand, I made my way to the dance floor. "I can't believe I's married now." Serenity said sounding like she from the color purple. Swaying back and forth we were in our own zone until we heard Quin on the mic.

Quin

"Hey everyone, can I have your attention." Walking over to Trinity, I helped her up and led her to the center of the dance floor where Qua and sis was. Loosening my tie, I felt like I was chocking. I didn't want to be rejected. Getting down on one knee, Trinity started to cry. "Trinity, I know these last couple of weeks we haven't been seeing eye to eye. I haven't even been sleeping in our bed but what I do know is these last weeks have let me know that I can't see myself in this world without my better half. I know we have a lot of making up to do, I know I have a lot of ass kissing to do, and I want you to wear my last name. I want you to let me know when I am making a mistake. I want you to make me a better man. I want you to be my wife, my better half and the moon to my stars and I would love for you to say YASSSS."

'YASSSSSSSSSSS BABY I WOULD LOVE TO BE YOUR WIFE." I stood up and she jumped in my arms. Kissing me and hugging me so tight. Serenity and Qua came over and joined our hug along with ma and pops.

"I can't I believe I am bout to have two married sons. I couldn't ask for better women to become my daughters-in-law." Ma said with tears streaming down her face.

"Now that that's over lets party for my bro and sis. Open bar let's make this a night to remember." Starting the booty call hustle had everyone on the floor. Black people always had to have them hustles going.

"Can I have this dance ma." Reaching for her hands, I helped her up and led her to the dance floor. Swaying back and forth I kissed her on the kips. "I love you so much ma. I'm so fucking sorry for fucking you over."

"It's in the past now bae, I know you're a better man and the only man for me. I'm sorry for making you feel like you were less than a father when you're one of the best fathers that I know. You're good to me and Jr and I know you're going to spoil the fuck out of baby girl. I love you daddy." Leaning her head up I leaned down to meet her halfway and kissed her.

"Awh shit now, my favorite couple back." Serenity came over and hugged both of us.

"Can I have this dance sis." Nodding her head, she walked on the dance floor with me.

"You look beautiful sis, thank you for giving me this moment when it was all about you."

"You're welcome." Looking over at Trinity sipping her pop, Serenity looked back at me. "I'll do anything to see her smile. While Qua and my boys have my heart now, Trinity. Sincere and you have a piece of it to I love y'all. But know this, if you fuck up again. I'm going to kill you myself." Laughing at her I promised her I had my shit together now.

"I'm not tryna brag or nothing, but I'm dancing with the bride while the groom over there with a bottle in his hand." Slapping me on the back of my head Serenity laughed.

"Leave my Husband alone." She walked over to her husband and I went to Trinity who was sitting right next to him.

"IM MRS. QUADIR MUTHAFUCKING RICHARDSON." Serenity yelled making everybody double over in laughter.

"So, the kids going home with us and y'all flying out tonight right." Mama came over to hug all of us.

"Yeah ma, we gotta sneak away cause Jr and Nadir don't play when it comes to their mama. She can't go nowhere without them two big head ass boys."

"Okay we're about to leave and take all the kids with us. I love y'all." After making sure our pops, mom and kids got in the car safely, we went back to the reception and partied.

Serenity

Laid out on the beach in the Bahamas I admired my ring Qua took a business call. This personal beach house that we had was wonderful. We had a personal beach in the back because we bought everything out. So, you know that I was out here ass naked letting the sunshine on my dark skin.

"Look I'm on my honeymoon with my wife, everything's going through Quin right now. Don't call my fucking phone no more until I call you." Qua was going off on whoever was on the opposite side of that phone. Standing up I walked up to him, wrapped my hands around him and put my hands in his swimming trunks. Massaging him slowly, I placed kisses on his back making him drop his phone. Turning around he wrapped his arounds around me and kissed me. Dropping down to my knees I pulled his dick out and deep throated him.

"Wait fuck ma." I knew what I was doing, I had my husband knees buckling. Sitting in the sand, I continued to suck him with my ass in the air. He reached around me and started thumbing my clit while slipping two fingers inside me. "Grrrrr, fuck." Pulling me up, he put us in the sixty-nine position, and attacked my clit. Taking him back in my mouth I sucked on the tip while two hand twisting the base. I felt myself about to cum so I picked up my pace so he could cum with me. When I felt him start growing in my mouth, I sucked the tip one more time and he exploded in my mouth. Like the good and nasty wife I was I swallowed it than sucked it to get him back hard. "Bae, wait a minute damn."

"We going all night daddy." Standing up, I mounted him, and he filled me up. Twirling my hips slowly I started bouncing slowly on him. "Siri play Beyond *Rocket*.

> *let me sit this ass on you show you how i feel let me take this off will you watch me yes, mass appeal don't take your eyes don't take your eyes off it watch it, babe if you like you can touch me baby do you do you wanna touch me baby, ooh grab a hold, don't let go let me know that you ready (ready) I just wanna show you now slow it down go around you rock*

Looking down at my husband biting his lip while I was riding him made me cum all over him but that still didn't stop me. When Megan the Stallion Cash Shit started playing, I turned around with his dick still inside me and started going dumb twerking all over him. Grabbing my hips, he stopped me and laid me in the sand on my back.

"Damn ma, I'm supposed to be making love to you on our honeymoon and you out here fucking the shit out of me." I put my arms around his neck pulling him in for a kiss.

"Give me your daughter." Sliding back inside me he started to stroke me slow and hard. Sliding all the way in and pulling out just to the tip then slamming back in. "ouuuuu daddy, just like that." I could tell his nut was rising when he started to make love to me with his face in the crock of my neck. Y'all ever been fucked so good that all you could do was lay there and moan and not say another word. Yeah, that's how my husband was making love to me right now.

"You gone give me my daughter ma." *Silence* "You gone give me my daughter Mrs. Richardson."

"Yassssss, daddy." I started squirting all over him as he filled me up with his kids. Picking me up he carried me into the beach house. Standing me up he filled the jacuzzi with hot water and added rose petals to it. While it filled up with water we went to rinse off in the shower before getting in the jacuzzi.

"Get settled in the jacuzzi while I go grab yo wine and my Hennessey." Doing as told I set in the hot water and through my head back. Not to long after my husband came back with wine, henny, blunts and fruit.

Sitting on the opposite side of me I placed my feet in his lap as he filled my glass with wine. He was the typical hood nigga because he turned his bottle all the way up.

"How you feelings Mrs. Richardson." I smiled at him lazily as he massaged my feet.

"I'm good, nothing in the world feels better than being yo Mrs." I moaned when he started to suck on my toes. Taking my seat on top of him again, I rode him until he begged me to stop.

Trinity

"Bae, can you bring a water and an apple please." I yelled to Quin before he came back into the room. It was closer to my due date and I was in so much pain. This little girl was kicking my ass and going crazy since her daddy was back. I guess this was her way of punishing me for keeping him away for them couple of weeks. As soon as he walked in, I stared at his fine ass. "Bae, please come put yo hands on my belly so she can calm the fuck down." Laughing he climbed behind me and rubbed on my belly.

"I missed you so much ma, little moments like this make me love you even more." He kissed my forehead as Quin Jr climbed on my belly and laid down.

"I missed you to baby. Please don't ever hurt me again and I promise that I will never hurt you again. I don't have a family, and it means everything to be building with you. I want to give my babies the life that I prayed for." Rubbing my son hair, I relaxed against my fiancé.

"Never, I never see myself hurting you again. When you told me we were over, I promise I wanted to kill yo ass. You had me listening to Toni Braxton and shit. Had serenity little ass about to kick my ass, I don't want no smoke with sis and behind you she wants all the fucking smoke. Period Pooh." I couldn't help but chuckle at his silly ass.

"Period Pooh. I want all the smoke behind her ass to. That's my baby Serenity and Sincere is my babies, I'll lay my life down and die for them."

"I know, but I'll lay my life down and die for all of y'all and that's real." Turning my head, I kissed him. We stayed like this for the rest of the day, this is what I always wanted, and I'd be damned if I let a trick ass bitch come between us.

"But bae, I got a question for real." He looked at me and I finished talking before he could say something. "What's up with you and strippers. You met me at a strip club, and you cheated on me with a stripper."

"I'm bouta stop you right there, yeah you were a stripper but not cause you had to be. You and Serenity ass own the fucking spot and was still stripping and shaking y'all asses in that bitch.

Qua 4 Months Later

Walking up the stairs I stopped by the twin's room and just admired my sons. They was the splitting image of me and Quin and that shit scared me something different. I know most niggas pass the torch to their sons, but I didn't want my sons or my nephews to be in the streets like me and Quin. My little niggas were gone go to college and be something. Kissing my boys on the cheek I walked down the hall to me and Serenity room. When I didn't see her in there, I walked to the room that we made her dressing room and watched as she swayed back and forth rubbing her round belly singing to herself in the mirror. She was now three months pregnant with twins again, Ya boy knocked her again. We were hoping for twin girls but the way she carrying, it's probably triplets in there. Lyfe Jennings *Must be nice* was blaring through her beats pill speaker.

Having someone who sticks around when the rough times get thick someone whose smile is bright enough to make the projects feel like a mansion must be nice having someone who loves you despite your faults must be nice having someone who talks the talk but also walks the walk must be nice having someone who understands that a thug has feelings too

Walking up behind her I put my big hands on her stomach and swayed side to side with her while looking in her eyes smiling. This woman was my whole fucking world, it's true what they say when a man finds a wife, he finds himself a good thing. Turning around she put her hands around my neck, and I leaned down to kiss her.

"Happy birthday Mr. Richardson. I love you daddy."

"Thank you, Mrs. Richardson, I love you more mama. Yo ass need to hurry up and finish so we can drop the kids off at mom and pops house." Slapping her on the ass she turned around and finished putting on her makeup on. Reaching around her I grabbed one of her makeup wipes and started wiping it off. "You don't need this ma, just put on yo lip gloss and lets go." I could have sworn I seen her dark ass blush.

"You right bae, you lucky its yo birthday though because I almost cussed yo ass out. But, I got you baby. We don't have to drop the babies off mom and pops are coming over here to get them and Quin and Trinity are coming over here too. Go smoke you a blunt while I go make sure the babies good." Kissing me one more time she walked out the dressing room. Walking into our bedroom I grabbed one of our premade blunts and walked out on the balcony. Leaning over the rail, I just stared into clouds. I was really married and getting out the fucking game. I remember the first time I seen My wife fine ass.

When shorty dropped into a split then made direct eye contact with me, my shit instantly bricked up. Down boy! Down boy! Shorty was the finest bitch in here and her fucking body was stacked. What surprised me the most is when she walked over to me and started grinding that big ass of her on my already hard dick, I know she felt that shit. She the type of chick I loved, the type that was confident and knew exactly what the hell she wanted.

My bad y'all let me tell you who the fuck I am. I'm Quadir Richardson, king of Chicago along with my Twin bro Quincy. We took over when our pops retired three years ago but a lot has changed since then. Niggas knew who the fuck we were because I wasn't scared to kill a nigga for looking at me wrong and Quincy was cold with his knives. He was the only nigga I knew who could throw a knife and kill a muthafucka from a mile away. Back to shorty though, grabbing her hips, she looked back at me and smiled.

"You like what you see daddy?" Without answering her I put a whole stack in the thong and shorty started going crazy.

"Aye bro let me find out you falling in love with a strip Bitch." Quincy laughed while slapping hands with me. I lowkey forgot this nigga was here.

"Party over daddy." She leaned over me and kissed me cheek and walked away leaving me hypnotized switching her big ass.

"Aye bro I think I just found my fucking match, shawty nice." Taking a shot of Henny to the head, I scanned the floor to see if I saw her, but shorty disappeared.

"I'm in love with a stripper looking ass nigga. Wait till I tell pops his son fell in love with a bitch who showing her ass for money. Nigga get the fuck outta here. Sick in love ass."

"You always joking around, I can't stand yo ugly ass bro."

"Bitch you look just like me." The look on his face was fucking priceless.

"Fuck you, Q." I had to laugh at his dumb ass because his was spitting the truth. This ugly black muthafucka looked just like my black ass.

"Happy birthday bro." Quin's voice snapped me out of my thoughts when he put his arm around my shoulder.

"Happy birthday bro." We gave each other a brotherly hug. "We really getting out the fucking game bro."

"I know man and this all I know, I can't even lie I'm gone miss the thrill I got from being one of the best fucking drug dealers, and murking niggas." If I wouldn't have known better, I'd say I seen my brothers eyes water up.

"Nigga is you about to cry?" I bumped his shoulder.

"Fuck you nigga, why the fuck would I cry?" Quin ass was doubled over laughing, his ass was to fucking goofy man. "Naw, for real bro, I'm so fucking proud of you. You the nigga I look up to when it comes to this being a man shit. Bro I wish I was half the man you were. You married with hella kids and you never stepped out on Serenity."

"Thanks bro, I'm proud of you to, I always thought when I got out the game yo ass was still gone be in it, but you proved me wrong. You and Trinity up Next twin."

"I'm proud of both of y'all ugly ass niggas." We turned around and our pops was standing in the door to the balcony. "Happy birthday sons, I'm so fucking happy y'all both made it to y'all thirties. Y'all niggas used to scare me when y'all was younger. I always thought I was gone have to bury one of my sons and that shit hunted me every day." He walked up and kissed both of us on our foreheads. I know y'all niggas probably thinking that shit gay but fuck y'all this our pops. "It's time to go celebrate. Let's go." Following our pops, we walked downstairs and Serenity, Trinity, our mom and kids was standing at the end of it.

As soon as we made it downstairs our mom jumped on us. "I'm so fucking proud of y'all, I remember I used to beg y'all daddy not to pass the torch to y'all but he just wouldn't listen. I've had plenty of nights when I couldn't sleep because I was scared one of y'all wouldn't make it back home to me. Quadir and Quincy you both have made your mother very proud, go celebrate."

"Happy birthday big bro." Trinity came and hugged me while Serenity went and hugged Quin. After kissing our kids, we walked out, and I'd be damned if these women of ours didn't have an Escalade Limo waiting on us.

"Let's get the party started Bihhhh, I ain't pregnant no more. Oh, shit sis you can't drink" Trinity stuck her tongue out and started twerking and grinding on Quin.

"Girl, fuck you." Serenity fake pouted. "Bae what you want to drink on."

"Grab me a bottle of Black Henny bae." Grabbing a whole bottle of black henny she opened it for me. "Damn bae, you treating me like a King."

"You are my king bae." Leaning over she kissed me and smiled.

"Why the fuck we going this way the lounge the other way." Quin just didn't have no type of home training.

"Bae, just ride we gone make it there. We got one more stop to make before we head to the club. Be like yo brother and just relax, here drink this black henny so I can get some henny dick tonight because I'm drinking Dussé and I'm trying to drive the boat." Trinity handed him a bottle of black henny, and he had this stupid ass grin on his face.

"Bae, they gone have as many kids as us in a couple more day's I guarantee you her ass gone get pregnant tonight." Serenity laughed while eating some grapes from the fruit tray.

"Why we at a hotel." As soon as I said that the doors opened, and King and Prince slid in with their women. "Ohhh shit my niggas wassup."

"Not shit, Happy birthday with y'all old asses." They grabbed they own bottle of black henny and started downing that shit.

"Thanks bro." It took us like thirty minutes to get to the lounge and when we pulled up it was packed as fuck, everybody came out to show love to us. Stepping out the limo couple by couple we walked down the red carpet.

"Qua, Quin, King, Prince Wassup my babies. I see y'all with y'all beautiful ass wives. Happy birthday Twins." The DJ was showing us made love. Walking through the lounge, the niggas was looking at our women and the bitches was drooling over us.

Making it through the crowd to get to the VIP section we finally set down and got it popping. "My nigga, we really 30 fucking years old. This shit is so fucking crazy." Quin was already drunk and Trinity was sitting on him twerking.

"You enjoying yoself baby." Serenity set on my lap and I hugged her around her waist.

"Yeah, you went all out for a nigga huh." I smirked at her through my low eyes because I was smoking some fat ass woods.

"Anything for my king. Y'all ready to make y'all speech." Nodding my head, I stood up and the men followed suit.

When the DJ seen us walk on stage, he handed Quin a mic and cut off the music. I was letting Quin make our departing speech.

"What's up y'all. Thank y'all for coming out and helping us celebrate our birthday and our departure from the game. This been a long twelve years. We been in this shit since we became legal. From the bitches to the niggas who tried to off us we stood tall through it all. This shit wouldn't have been possible without half of y'all niggas help. I know sometimes we was pushy and shit but we appreciate the fuck out of y'all. I never imagined me and my bro leaving the game but when we met these bad ass best friends our whole fucking world changed for the better. Trinity and Serenity come up here." After the girls came and stood by our sides he finished talking. "These two beautiful ass women changed me and my twin's life, before them we was some wild ass niggas who didn't give a fuck about nothing. But we have a purpose now, we family men and because of that we have to let this game go. King and Prince make y'all way to the stage." Again, he waited until they came to the stage. "These two niggas is just as hungry as me and my bro was at the age. They had our back through it all and never questioned our motions. Qua you want to do the honors." Handing me the mic he came and stepped by my side.

"King and Prince it's a honor to give you the keys to the muthafucking city. Not only the city but every other fucking city and state that we have. My niggas y'all deserve it." Everybody started clapping as me and Quin handed them keys to their new Bugatti's that was waiting outside for them.

Dapping them up we gave them brotherly hugs and walked off the stage as the music started to play again.

Serenity hugged me tight and kissed me. "It's all over bae. You're officially a businessman."

"It's all over ma. We can only go up from here." Kissing her I looked over and seen Trinity and Quin hugging and she was crying just like Serenity was. Looking over to King and Prince I nodded at them. This shit was finally over, it was all about my family now. Don't cry y'all, our story over but Kings and Princes is just starting.

King

IT'S ROYALTY SEASON NOW BITCH. Catch us in King and Prince *The takeover.*

King and Prince: The Takeover

Coming Soon

(Unedited)

What you doing with all that ass, let me touch, she said its mine so I smack it while I fuck it." Moneybagg YO and Megan The Stallion plays in the background as these two ass Red bones was sucking my dick. "Don't forget the balls bitch." My eyes rolled in the back of my head. These hoes was getting me right after the day had. Me and bro just came back from chi and these niggas thought shit was funny cause the game was ours. These niggas had us running around. We were more on the back burner and had to get our lieutenant together. Pulling up one of these freak bitches I bent her ass over with the perfect arch. Sliding the condom on these thick 11 inches, I eased it into her soaking wet pussy. This bitch had walls that sucked the shit out me.

"Damn bitch, I thought you wasn't going to have no walls." I told her before slapping her ass and watching it jiggle. Going in and out, hitting her with a long stroke. Watching red bone 2 come up on side of me and start slobbing on my balls at the same time almost made me nut.

"O bitch I feel them walls. You bout to cum huh." Speeding up I felt my nut rising, pulling out and snatching the condom off. I shot it off their face. going to the bathroom to take y shower. They can have the room for the rest of the night. After getting out the shower I through they ass a couple stacks and made my way out to the valet. He already had my car waiting. This nice as Bugatti that the twins got me had me feeling like the young price that I am. The inside was accustomed with crowns and shit. it was my favorite color, black.

Pulling up to my house, I pulled into the garage. My house wasn't as big as King's but it was made for me. walking in through the kitchen I took my shoes off before going to my bedroom and taking another shower. My house was the total package three bedrooms, three bathrooms, pool, jacuzzi and my man cave in the basement with the 70 inch and all my game systems hooked up. This was home even though I spent majority of my time with King and Kenzie. Jumping in my California king size bed, ass naked, I got under the covers until sleep found me.

Buzz buzz

Turning over hearing my phone buzz. I looked at the time, I had only been sleep a couple hours.

    Bro: Meet me at the crib

    Not bothering to text, him back I got up and brushed my teeth. Going to my closet I picked out my black True's and black thermal, just in case I had to go put in work. Locking up in my house I got in my car and was on my way. King lived about 20 minutes away from me, but I made it there in 10. Parking in the circular driveway. I used my key to gain entrance.

    "Who the fuck walking in my house?" I heard King yell front the living room.

    "Who the fuck else got keys to this bitch besides me and yo wife." I took my shoes off and made my way to where he was. Walking into the living room Kenzie had her legs on King while he was rubbing her feet and she was rubbing that big ass belly. Walking over to them I kissed Kenzie on the cheek and dapped up bro.

    "Sis, I think you got bigger since yesterday."

    "I feel like it. This lil girl got 5 weeks to vacate the premises. I need my body back."

"Don't be trying to kick my princess out early, let her finish baking." King told her while helping her stand up to give us some privacy. She didn't know nothing about business. King kept her away from the life style. Now don't get me wrong, she knew how to buss guns in worst case scenarios but, the police would never be able to implement he in anything.

Making sure that she was out of ear shot. King and I got down to business. "Bro that nigga Ace going to be a problem. He starting to recruit our niggas that we have on payroll. Trell told me that he seen him around the house a lot lately when he thought He wasn't there. This man thinks that he about to snatch what we been building. He was nothing but trying to make money."

"This shit pissing the fuck off. We need a meeting now. Send that shit out. Everyone need to be at the warehouse tonight." I was pissed off to the max. walking outside leaving King in the house, I sparked my blunt up. I needed something to calm my nerves. This nigga was playing with the right ones. I guess its tru you can't leave niggas like him alive.

"PRINCE. PRINCE PRINNNNCCCCCEEEE" I heard King calling my name. I threw the blunt down and ran in the house. He was coming down the stairs with a limp Kenzie.

"What the fuck happened."

"I don't know just grab yo keys and let's roll." Running out the house I slipped on King house shoes, I didn't have time to put no shoes on. Opening the door for King he jumped in with the driver side and pushed this bitch doing 100 mph. I made it to Genesys Hospital. Running in the ER I grabbed the first Dr I seen.

Doc I need you now my sis unconscious and she 8 months pregnant.

"Nurse grab a gurney and follow me." Running outside King was at the door kicking it in, it wasn't opening fast enough for him. Laying her on the gurney we started following into the doctor told us we had to wait right there.

Coming soon King and Prince

The Take Over

Made in United States
Orlando, FL
18 January 2024